He touched her shoulder lightly. "Did you plan on sleeping in this dress?"

Dana swallowed hard. "Well, you can unbutton the top two buttons. That ought to get me started."

Ben laughed softly, then touched the low-cut edge of the back of her gown. Her breath caught. When he undid the top button, his knuckles brushed the newly exposed skin. When he reached for the next button and the next, she closed her eyes, wishing he'd meant to set off the heat building inside her.

"This isn't what I expected when I promised to take care of you, but I won't complain." He slid his hand into the unbuttoned back of her gown, pressing his fingers, wide and firm, against her. The soft material slipped down her shoulder. Goose bumps rippled along her skin.

To accompany the chill running down her spine.

"Take care…?" she repeated.

"Of you *and* the kids."

She tried to keep her tone even, her voice soft. "And who did you make that promise to?"

He shifted, as if her question made him uncomfortable. A small gap opened between them, and her body cooled.

"Paul," he said.

"Then it has to stop. As I've told you so many times I've lost count, I can take care of myself—and my children." She tugged the lace overskirt of her gown into place. "And I think it's time for you to go."

Dear Reader,

I'm so glad to have the chance to tell you Ben Sawyer's story, because it would *not* leave me alone.

When his best friend dies, Ben is obligated to take care of his friend's family. He's desperate to do the right thing…yet he has spent his life since kindergarten longing for the woman he now must watch over.

Thanks to the local matchmakers and a plan of his own, he and Dana are forced together. But his plan backfires, and he learns the awful truth in the saying "Be careful what you wish for."

Now that Dana is within his reach, propriety and honor and a promise he made all keep him from stepping over the line. From claiming the one woman meant for him.

Writing this book, I found myself holding my breath as I waited for this honorable man to find a solution to his dilemma. I hope you find your breath catching, too, as you read this story.

Please let me know what you think of it! You can reach me at P.O. Box 504 Gilbert, AZ 85299 or through my website, www.barbarawhitedaille.com. I'm also on Facebook: www.facebook.com/barbarawhitedaille and Twitter: https://twitter.com/BarbaraWDaille.

All my best to you.

Until we meet again,

Barbara White Daille

Honorable Rancher

BARBARA WHITE DAILLE

HARLEQUIN®
entertain, enrich, inspire™

Recycling programs
for this product may
not exist in your area.

ISBN-13: 978-0-373-75420-5

HONORABLE RANCHER

ABOUT THE AUTHOR

Barbara White Daille lives with her husband in the sunny Southwest, where they don't mind the lizards in their front yard but could do without the scorpions in the bathroom.

A writer from the age of nine and a novelist since eighth grade, Barbara is now an award-winning author with a number of novels to her credit.

When she was very young, Barbara learned from her mom about the storytelling magic in books—and she's been hooked ever since. She hopes you will enjoy reading her books and will find your own magic in them!

She'd also love to have you drop by and visit her at her website, www.barbarawhitedaille.com.

Books by Barbara White Daille

HARLEQUIN AMERICAN ROMANCE

1131—THE SHERIFF'S SON
1140—COURT ME, COWBOY
1328—FAMILY MATTERS
1353—A RANCHER'S PRIDE
1391—THE RODEO MAN'S DAUGHTER

In memory of F. D. White

an honorable man himself

and

as always, to Rich,

the best man for me

~~~~~~

I reckon there are many ways

to call a man a hero.

Chapter One

Always a bridesmaid, never a bride.

Ben Sawyer had heard folks say that of some women. Not the one standing on the far side of the banquet hall from him, though. The one who'd done her best all day to avoid him.

Dana Wright had once worn a long white gown and walked down the aisle to meet her groom. *He* should know, as he'd stood up near the altar holding the ring his best friend would slip onto her finger.

Now, if the saying held true for the male side of a wedding party, he surely fit the bill.

Always a groomsman, never a groom.

Always losing out.

No sense worrying over it. He'd made his decisions a long time ago. Still, he had to fight to keep his eyes from tracking Dana's every move.

Twirling the stem of his champagne glass in his fingers, he watched the couples two-stepping past him. After plenty of turns on the dance floor himself this evening, he'd decided to sit this one out. Every once in a while, in a gap between the couples, he could see the opposite side of the hall. Just then, he caught sight of Dana disappearing through one of the glass doors to the terrace.

The newlyweds danced toward him.

"Having fun yet?" Tess asked.

"Absolutely," he confirmed. "Like everyone else."

Except Dana?

Tess's groom, Caleb, swept her away.

Ben set his glass on a nearby waiter's tray and began circling the room. Every few feet, someone stopped him. While he always enjoyed a good conversation, the interruptions came more often than he would've liked right now.

Finally, he eased away from a small group and edged over to the doorway Dana had exited through.

In the light from the carriage lamps outside, he saw her standing alone near one of the stone fountains flanking the club's entrance. He frowned and went through the door, pulling it closed behind him without a sound.

Her back to the building, she stared down into the water pooling in the base of the fountain. Lamplight and moonlight combined to make the silver combs in her blond hair sparkle. The combs held her hair up, exposing the smooth, pale skin of her neck. A row of buttons that matched her long pink dress marched down to the point where a bunch of lacy fabric covered the sweet curves of her hips.

His mouth went dry. He'd have welcomed another glass of champagne at the moment. Hell, he needed it to wet his tight throat. To occupy his hands. His fingers itched to touch those buttons now taunting him.

How had she managed to get into that dress all by herself? Would she need a hand getting out of it?

He shook his head at the stupidity—and the futility—of his questions. Of his dreams. Nine-year-old Lissa had probably buttoned her mother's dress and would unbutton it, too. In any case, Dana certainly wouldn't want his help. She didn't want his assistance with anything.

That gave him trouble, in view of the promise he'd made to his best friend. A promise he aimed to keep.

For a moment, he stood there considering his next move. Unusual for him. Folks teased that he'd talk to a tree if he couldn't find a person handy to listen to him. Yet, for the first time in his life, he didn't know what to say.

He took a deep breath and let it out again. Not wanting to startle her, he called her name in a low tone.

Without turning to look, she raised her chin a notch. She'd recognized his voice and gone into defensive mode. Hadn't he known she would? The sight should have made him turn around and leave. Instead, he smiled.

He never could pass up a challenge.

He ambled across the open space to stand by her side. Her head barely reached his shoulder. He caught the faint scent of a flowery perfume. When she neither lowered her chin nor looked at him, he gestured toward one of the small stone benches near the fountain. "How about you relax and we call a truce for tonight? After all, we're here to celebrate with Tess and Caleb."

She glanced from the bench to the country club as if assessing the lesser of two evils. "You're right, it's their night." With a small sigh, she took a seat.

The bench proved narrower than he'd expected and put him closer to her than he should've risked, truce or no truce. Their arms touched. Their elbows bumped. It would have made sense for him to wrap his arm around her shoulders. They were friends, weren't they? But once he'd touched her, could he keep it at that?

Her expression softened. "Caleb went all out for Tess, didn't he?"

"Renting the biggest hall within a hundred miles of Flagman's Folly? I'll say. Good of him to invite all the folks from town to the wedding, too."

"He seemed surprised that everyone accepted. But I

know they wanted to wish him and Tess well." She smiled softly. "Tess makes a beautiful bride."

You did, too. Without missing a beat, he changed the words that had come so quickly to him. "You're looking good in that maid of honor dress yourself."

"Matron," she said. "Being a widow makes me a matron of honor."

Which makes you a woman alone with three little kids. So, why won't you accept my help? He couldn't ask that tonight. Not after he'd called for a ceasefire between them. He probably wouldn't ask that ever, as nine times out of ten, the shots came from Dana's side of their conversations. She'd never acted so defensively with him before Paul died.

"What is it they're calling Nate again?" he asked. Nate was the bride and groom's nine-year-old tomboy and the best buddy of Dana's daughter Lissa. Like the girls, Tess and Dana had been best friends all through school.

"A junior bridesmaid." She laughed. "Nate stopped fighting over wearing a dress the minute Caleb said he'd get her a pair of boots made to match his. She held her ground about being a flower girl, though."

He chuckled. "That sounds like her. Well, Sam's little girl had a good time dropping those petals in the church aisle. I heard you made her dress. And yours. Nice."

Damn him for using the compliment, but it gave him a reason to touch her lacy pink sleeve.

She shied like a filly come eye to eye with a rattler.

He clasped his hands together and stared down at them.

When he looked at her profile again, he found her gazing into the distance, unblinking. The moonlight showed her lips pressed together in a straight line, the way he'd noted much too often lately. Her cheekbones had never looked sharp before now.

Nothing could make her less beautiful to him, but it shocked him to realize she had lost weight.

She'd driven herself after losing Paul. Trying to handle everything alone *had* to be too much for her. He needed to stop thinking about himself—about what he wanted and could never have—and figure out some way to be of help to her.

He'd already bought the building where she rented office space so he could give her a break on the rent. There had to be something else he could do.

Right now, he just needed to get her talking. He cleared his dry throat. "Caleb's fired up about his new property. I've got to hand it to you for that one. Nobody could've done a better job of selling that ranch, especially considering it's bigger than every spread around here."

She waved her hand as if to brush his words away. "That was Tess's effort, mostly. I just stepped in to handle the paperwork when we knew she'd become half owner. Besides, she had to focus on getting married."

"Whatever the reason, I know she was happy to have you help wrap everything up in time for the wedding."

He knew Dana accepted help in return from Tess, too, when she needed it. Why wouldn't she take it from him? They'd all been friends forever, through high school and beyond. Not Caleb, who at some point had fallen a year behind. But he and Tess and Dana. Sam Robertson. Paul Wright.

He thought of his best buddy often, recalling him as young and full of life. As part of almost every memory he'd forged since the day he started school. He tried not to think about Paul's death a year and a half ago. Impossible to avoid that thought at the moment, with the man's widow sitting on the cold stone bench beside him.

In all the years since grade school, nothing had ever

come between Paul and Dana. He had always honored that. Now he had to make doubly sure not to cross the line. "Today has to be hard for you," he said, keeping his voice low.

"Seeing Tess and Caleb so happy? Why should that cause me any trouble? I'm glad they're finally together."

She meant it, he knew, though her words sounded as brittle as the chipped ice in the banquet hall's champagne buckets. In the moonlight, her eyes glittered. Had she tried for a lighter tone to fight back tears? Or to prove how comfortable she felt around him?

Why did she have to prove anything? Why the heck couldn't she enjoy his company, the way she always used to? If she'd just give him that, he'd feel satisfied.

Sure, he would.

She'd grown quiet again, and he gestured toward the fountain. "What brought you out here? Wanting to make a wish?"

She shook her head. "No. Those are for people who aren't willing to work hard to get what they want."

"I can't argue with you there." Still, he felt tempted to toss a coin into the water for a wish of his own—that for once, she'd let him make things easier for her. "But there's such a thing as working too hard, you know."

"Ben, please." She gathered up her dress and stood. "You called the truce yourself, remember? I know you only want to help. For Paul. And because we're *friends*." Her voice shook from her stress on the word. "We've had this conversation before. Now, once and for all, I'm doing fine." As if to prove her point, she smiled. "And I have to go inside. Tess will be tossing her bouquet soon. I wouldn't want to lose out on that."

A tear sparkled at the corner of her eye.

Missing the chance to catch a handful of flowers couldn't

upset her that much. He knew what she really missed—having a husband by her side. Her husband.

His best friend.

But neither of them would have Paul back in their lives.

Before he could get to his feet, she left, running away like that princess in the fairy tale his niece asked him to read to her over and over again.

No, not a princess. The one who took off without her glass slipper—Cinderella.

Dana was no Cinderella. She hadn't left a shoe behind. Hadn't even dropped a button from that pink dress as something for him to remember her by. As if he could ever forget her.

She'd been the heroine of a story he'd once created long ago, a story he'd had to write in his head because he hadn't yet known how to spell all the words.

How did it go? Like in his niece's storybook…

Once upon a time, that was it.

Once upon a time, in the Land of Enchantment—otherwise known as the state of New Mexico—Benjamin Franklin Sawyer had high hopes and a huge crush on the girl who sat one desk over from him in their classroom every day.

No other girl in town, Ben felt sure, could beat Dana Smith, and most likely no other woman in the world could compare to her, either. In any case, without a doubt, she was the cutest of all his female friends in their kindergarten classroom.

Unfortunately, when the teacher moved his best friend, Paul Wright, to the desk on the other side of Dana's, Ben saw his hopes dashed.

The crush, however, continued. For a good long while.

As for Benjamin Franklin Sawyer's hopes…

Well, not every story had a happy ending.

Not even Dana's.

Since Paul's death, they had seen less and less of each other. By her choice, not his.

She needed time, he had told himself. Needed space. So he'd waited. He'd talked himself down. He'd exercised every horse in his stable enough to cover every inch of the land he owned. When none of that worked, he'd bought the danged office building. And even that hadn't brought him peace.

Seeing her now had.

He never could stand to watch her cry, but tonight, he welcomed those tears in her eyes and the way she'd hurried away from him. *Doing fine,* she'd said. Like hell. Her actions revealed more than she would willingly tell him. More than she'd ever want him to know.

She needed his help, though she refused to accept it.

The help he had promised Paul he would give her.

No matter how firmly she dug her heels in and how often she turned him down, he was damned well going to keep that promise.

AFTER ONE LAST BREATH of fresh air to calm herself, Dana slipped back into the banquet hall and sought safety at one of the tables.

"Hey, Dana, over here!"

Even above the music, she heard the familiar voice and fought to hide her cringe of dismay.

No safety for her tonight, anywhere.

Forcing a smile, she hurried toward the table halfway around the dance floor. Anything to keep from standing near the door. If Ben found her there, he would assume she had waited for him.

For the past year and more, she had done just the opposite—tried her best to keep out of his way. A ridiculous goal in a town the size of Flagman's Folly, where you couldn't step out your front door without meeting some-one you knew.

Then he'd bought the building that housed her office, and she'd had to work twice as hard to avoid him. Ten times as hard to ignore her feelings. Because it wasn't only anger and irritation that made her insist she was fine. And that had sent her running from him now.

Reaching the table, she smiled down at Tess's aunt Ella-mae. "Everything okay?" she asked. "Did you need some-thing?"

"Everything's fine," the older woman said.

Fine. That word again. She resisted the urge to steal a backward glance at the French doors. To look for Ben.

They'd been friends forever, yet she couldn't risk being near him anymore. Talking with him meant she had to raise her guard. Trying to make him understand how she felt made her frustrated, in more ways than she wanted to think about. Every time they spoke to each other, she left more shaken than before.

Even tonight, when she fled outside for a few minutes alone, she'd found no escape from him. Worse, sitting be-side him in the moonlight, she'd had trouble catching her breath. And that had nothing to do with the formfitting bodice of her gown.

"We were wondering what you'd gotten up to," Ella-mae said.

She jumped. "Up to? Nothing. I'm the matron of honor, that's all. It's a busy job."

"Yeah. So, it's funny you found time to run off like that."

Ellamae's weatherworn face and gruff tone made most kids in town antsy around her. Her job as court clerk only increased their anxiety. But like a prickly pear cactus, her rough exterior covered the softness beneath.

Years of spending time around Tess's family had taught

Dana that. She could handle Ellamae. "I just went out for a quick breath of fresh air."

"Not so quick, was it?"

She blinked. On the other hand, the woman's tendency to see all and want to know all made *her* a bit antsy, too.

Especially when she had so much to hide.

The man on Ellamae's other side broke in. "Glad you're back, anyhow," Judge Baylor said. "Wouldn't want to miss Tess throwing out her bouquet."

"Oh, I think I'll pass."

The judge's bright blue eyes met hers. "Well, now. Can't have you doing that, can we? It's tradition."

As Ellamae nodded vigorously, the bandleader made the announcement. At the tables around them, women jumped up from their seats.

Knowing enough not to protest, Dana swallowed a sigh. Everyone had respected her year and more of mourning, but with the folks of Flagman's Folly, tradition was practically the law. And between them, Ellamae and the judge *were* the law in town.

"Time you got back into the swing of things," Ellamae said.

Trust her to speak her mind. She now shooed Dana into the crowd with as much enthusiasm as little Becky Robertson shooed her chickens into their new coop.

Giving up, Dana joined the women surging toward the dance floor. Laughter broke out from behind her, and she looked back.

Ellamae stood waving a well-used baseball catcher's mitt. She hurried to Dana's side. "C'mon, girl, let's move it. I got done out of catching the bouquet at Sam Robertson's wedding, but I'm not missing a chance at this one."

Almost the same words Dana had used to escape from Ben. Time to make good on her excuse. Refusing to look for him, she took her spot with the women. From the middle of the crowd, Lissa and Nate turned, grinning, to wave at her. She waved back.

Ellamae nudged her, making elbow room.

Dana laughed and edged a few steps away. Though she stayed on the fringes, she held her hands up as everyone else did and matched their wide smiles.

The bride listened to her guests, all telling her how and when and where to toss her bouquet. Dana knew each woman in the group hoped to become the lucky winner—especially Ellamae, who stood waving her mitt-clad hand above her head.

Good luck to her. And to anyone else on that dance floor.

As long as she stayed behind all the other women, the bouquet shouldn't come anywhere near her. Just the idea that she might win the toss made her heart thud painfully.

Unable to stop herself, she glanced across the room. Ben stood near the French doors, gazing at her, and she hurriedly turned away. Knowing he watched only made things worse.

The sigh she swallowed bordered on a sob. Of all the folks in town who worried her, good old Ben topped the list. Not only because he kept offering to help her.

But because he would be the person most hurt by the secrets she kept.

"Everybody set?" Tess called.

The crowd murmured in anticipation, and Dana forced herself to focus. If she didn't, it would be just her luck not to realize the bouquet had come right at her until too late—after her reflexes had kicked in and she had caught it.

Tess swung her arm as if winding up for a baseball pitch, then let the flower arrangement fly. It skimmed the fingertips of one woman after another, bouncing its way across the crowd.

To the amusement of everyone in the hall, Ellamae made

a valiant effort to snag the bouquet in midair. The cumbersome baseball mitt let her down. The flowers slipped from her grasp, tumbled in Dana's direction, bounced off her shoulder, and landed in the arms of five-year-old Becky Robertson, who squealed. Jaw dropped and eyes wide, she looked up at Dana.

Sam's little girl was deaf. Glad his wife had taught folks some sign language, Dana fluttered her hands in the air, using the gesture for applause. Hearing Becky's high-pitched laugh made her smile. Dana held her right hand palm turned inward a couple of inches from her own face. Tilting her hand, she pulled all her fingertips together. *"Pretty."*

Clutching the bouquet, Becky nodded energetically, then ran toward her daddy, who waited at the edge of the dance floor.

"There goes one happy young'un," Ellamae said, shaking her head. "Well, after seeing that smile, guess I can't begrudge the girl. Better luck next time for the rest of us."

Not for me, Dana thought with relief as the other women drifted away and Ellamae stomped off in a pretend sulk. Her good fortune had come from *not* getting stuck with that bouquet.

Then she made the mistake of looking at Ben. No smiles there. No luck for her, either. He had started across the room toward her.

Chapter Two

Had Ben read her thoughts in her face from all the way across the room? Had everyone in the entire banquet hall noticed her relief at not catching the bouquet?

Casually, she hoped, Dana glanced away from Ben at the tables clustered around the dance floor. No one seemed to pay any special attention to her—except the bride, who marched up, shaking her head. "What in the world do you call that attempt? You didn't even try to catch it."

"I most certainly did. Ellamae made me nervous."

"Yeah, I'll bet." Tess frowned. "Are you having a good time?"

"Of course."

"I wonder. I wish we could have matched you up with a more eligible partner."

"Don't be silly. Sam and I are perfectly happy to act as a couple for the day."

Tess laughed. "You know, Caleb planned to ask him to stand up for him anyhow, but Sam beat him to it. He insisted Caleb choose him. Since he'd just gotten married, Sam claimed he would be the *best* best man Caleb could ever find."

No, he wouldn't. Dana had to bite her tongue to keep the words from spilling out. Of all the males in the room,

Ben Sawyer would make the best man. He'd proven that ever since her own wedding. And in all the years before it.

He'd always been there for her, had always played such a big role in her life. Right now, though, she felt sure he planned to steal the show. Or at least, to make a scene. One she didn't want Tess to witness.

"Speaking of Caleb," she said quickly, "he's trying to get your attention." She gestured toward Tess's new husband, who had pulled a chair into the middle of the dance floor.

Tess gave an exaggerated groan. "Oh, no. It's garter time." She murmured, "Tradition is all well and good, but we have to draw the line somewhere. I've got the garter around my ankle." She grinned. "I hope he's not too disappointed."

Dana forced a laugh. "You have no worries there." The band played a few bouncy chords. Copying Ellamae, she made shooing motions toward Tess. "Go on. Everyone's waiting."

Single males, including Ben, flowed onto the dance floor. But as Tess returned to the front of the hall, he broke from the group and veered toward Dana.

"Did Tess tell you what she thought about your pathetic try at that bouquet?" he asked.

She exhaled in exasperation. They certainly had an audience now. She caught several people watching them, including Judge Baylor, who had taken pride of place in the center of the floor.

If she had to, she would smile until her cheeks hurt. But she wouldn't take a lecture from Ben. "Yes, Tess gave me her feedback. So I won't need any from you. Thanks, anyway."

"But I had my entire speech planned."

She laughed. "Save it for someone else. And for your information, as I told Tess, Ellamae made me back off."

His brows rose. "That's a switch." He smiled as if to soften his words. "I thought you could handle anyone who got in your way."

"Anyone but you, Ben," she muttered after he'd left to rejoin the other men.

At the front of the room, teasing his blushing bride, the groom tugged at the hem of her gown. As the other wedding guests cheered him on, Dana's mind wandered—directly to the dark-haired man whose shoulders strained the fabric of his well-cut tuxedo.

After Paul's death, Ben had offered to do anything he could to make things easier for her. His attention smothered her. His kindhearted attempts to help threatened to do even more. To make her needy and dependent and weak.

She couldn't let that happen. Not after all the years she'd heard those words from another man—the one she had mistakenly married. Paul had forced those words on her, had done his best to convince her they truly described her. She couldn't fall for that again, either.

And so, it had been easiest—best—to turn away from Ben. To *stay* away from him, when she wanted to do just the opposite. When everything in her longed for—

Laughter rippled around her. She sagged in relief, genuinely glad for the interruption that kept her from going down that mental road. She couldn't go anywhere with Ben. Shouldn't even think about him.

Outside, alone with him in the moonlight, sitting beside him on that bench, she'd wanted just to close her eyes and lean against him and see what would happen next. But she couldn't. Too many responsibilities and too many bad memories would keep her from ever relying on any man again.

Especially Ben.

As if she had called his name, he turned. Her breath

caught. It wasn't until he approached her that she realized the garter toss had ended.

The music changed from the bouncy rhythm to a slower beat.

"May I have this dance?" he asked. He stood so tall, she had to look up to see his dark eyes staring down at her.

At the thought of stepping into his arms, her heart lurched. A dangerous road… A risky decision…

Somehow, she had escaped having to dance with him at Sam and Kayla's wedding the year before. She had managed to avoid that tonight, too. Until now. But they had an audience all around—all the folks from Flagman's Folly—scrutinizing their every move.

She blurted the only thing that came to mind. "Why not? We're friends, aren't we?"

His expression solemn, he nodded and held out his hand.

She couldn't have refused his invitation. Couldn't have turned him down. And he knew it. Of course, the matron of honor would dance with the ushers, too.

Why was she trying to kid herself? She wouldn't have turned Ben away at all.

But she should have.

He took her hand and settled his free arm around her waist, holding her in a light but steady embrace. As he led her expertly around the crowded floor, she tried desperately to focus on her movements. One trip over her own feet, and she'd make a fool of herself. One slip on this dance floor, and she'd wind up even closer to him than she stood now.

If that were possible.

She was nearly nestled against him. Her head swam, and she strained to keep her focus on the lapel of his dark tuxedo. She would not look up at him. She would not meet his eyes. She was too afraid of what he would read in hers.

There were other senses besides sight, though.

His warmth enveloped her, relaxing her even as it made her heart beat triple-time.

Loving the scent of his spicy aftershave, she inhaled deeply…and caught herself just as her eyelids began to close. Wouldn't that have made a pretty picture for all the wedding guests to see!

She shifted slightly in his arms. Her hand brushed the edge of his collar, her fingertip catching the faint sandpaper prickle of five-o'clock shadow on his neck. A shiver ran through her.

"You okay?" he murmured, tilting his head down.

"Fine," she whispered. So many uses for that one little word. So many lies.

He moved his arm from around her waist and rested his hand flat against her back. His thumb grazed the skin left exposed by her gown. For a moment, she felt sure he'd done it deliberately.

Silly wishful thinking. Yet she had to swallow hard against the small, strangled sound that had risen to the back of her throat. She *should* have turned him down.

No matter how much she longed for him to hold her.

The musicians brought the song to an end. With a sigh of relief, she dropped her arms and stepped back. Instantly, she missed his warmth.

"Thank you for the dance," he said.

Reluctantly she looked up, more unwilling than ever to meet his eyes. Instead, she focused on his mouth. On any other man she might have taken the curve of those lips as a complacent smile. Or even a self-satisfied smirk.

Not on Ben.

"Thank you, too," she murmured. She saw Tess approaching and turned to her.

"Dana, didn't you say P.J. and Stacey are staying with Anne all night?"

"Yes." The casual question helped clear her head. She had made special arrangements with her babysitter. "Anne's keeping them at her house, since I knew Lissa and I would get home so late."

"Good. But Lissa's now staying at the Whistlestop with Nate."

Dana frowned. Tess's mother had turned their family home into a bed-and-breakfast inn a couple of years earlier. Lissa spent the night at the Whistlestop Inn as often as Nate stayed at their house. But... "Roselynn doesn't need an extra—"

"No buts, please. I checked with Mom first." Tess leaned toward them and continued in a lower voice, "Nate's having a hard time adjusting to us going away. I invited Lissa."

"In that case, then, of course."

"Great." Tess turned to Ben. "We've had to do some rearranging and the limo's now overflowing. You won't mind taking Dana back to town, will you?"

"Of course not."

"But—" Dana started.

"Gotta run," Tess interrupted. Again. "Caleb's waiting." She turned away, her gown swirling behind her.

"I can find another ride—"

"No need," Ben said.

He closed his fingers around her elbow as if she planned to hurry after Tess. She did. "Duty calls," she said, tugging her arm free. "After all, I'm Tess's matron of honor tonight."

"No problem," he said easily. "I'll be waiting for you when it's time to go."

A few quick steps, and she'd left him behind. If only she could have left her own treacherous thoughts on the dance floor, too. On the long ride to Flagman's Folly in the quiet darkness of his truck, she'd better put those thoughts out of her mind. Or even safer, put herself to sleep. Then she wouldn't be tempted to think…to say…to do…anything she'd regret.

Silly to worry about that. What harm could come from a simple ride home with him?

Good old, dependable Ben. She could count on him to be there for her. To be her friend, always. To never do anything inappropriate.

It was enough to break her heart.

A RED GLEAM FROM THE ROAD up ahead caught Ben's eye. The headlamps of his pickup truck reflected off the taillights of a vehicle pulled to one side of the road.

"Ben," Dana said, her voice tight with concern.

"Nothing to worry about." Even if he hadn't seen the car days ago, he'd have realized that. The coating of yellow dust from bumper to bumper and the dingy handkerchief hanging from the antenna told him it had sat there for a while. "I noticed it when I came this way last week."

No need to check for anyone stranded inside the vehicle. Still, habits died hard. He slowed for a look as he drove past. Around here, with towns few and far apart and where the sun parched everything it touched, folks kept an eye out for others.

Just as he watched over Dana.

"I'm surprised you didn't notice it before tonight," he added. "You're on the road often enough."

"Not lately." She sounded irritated.

"In fact, that could've easily been your van broken down back there. And what would you have done by yourself?"

"Called for a tow truck, of course. Besides, when I leave town, I'm usually not alone. I have clients with me."

She shifted in the passenger seat.

She hadn't said much so far on their way home. He'd even

caught her with her eyes closed a few times. No surprise, considering the clock read ten past midnight.

Cinderella hadn't made it home on time.

Between her last-minute duties at the banquet hall and the long ride back to town, they'd only come to the outskirts of Flagman's Folly now.

"Sleep well?" he asked, smiling.

"Just resting my eyes."

In the dim light from the dashboard, he could see the line of her cheekbones. Again, he noted the weight she'd lost. Still, she looked beautiful. But tired. "With all the kids away, maybe you can get some extra rest in the morning."

"Not a chance. I'm picking up P.J. and Stacey at seven."

"So early?"

She laughed softly. "I wouldn't inflict P.J. on Anne and her mother any longer than that."

It had been a while since he'd seen the kids. Once, he'd had the run of Paul's house. He swallowed the bitter thought and kept his eyes on the road. "He's still a chatterbox, huh?"

"*Always been* a chatterbox," she corrected.

"He takes after his mama."

"He does not."

His laugh sounded much more loud than hers had. "Now, don't try pulling that one on me. I grew up with you, remember?"

"How could I forget?"

She didn't sound happy about it. "Was it that bad?"

"Don't be silly." She sighed. "I didn't mean that. I was just thinking in general about growing up here."

"The best place in the world," he said.

"Mmm."

"What? You don't agree?"

"Of course, I do. It's just…you know how people are here. *They* don't forget a thing, either."

"Works for me. It's nice to have folks around who know all about you." *Nice, except for their long list of expectations.* He stayed quiet for a while, listening to the tires whip the road. "Well," he said, finally, "I'd hate to live in a town where nobody knew his neighbor. Wouldn't you?"

She didn't answer. He smiled. She'd gone back to resting her eyes again. Her lashes left shadows on her cheeks. Her lips had softened. He wanted a taste. When he'd held her in his arms tonight, he'd had to fight like hell to keep from pulling her closer and kissing her.

Before they'd left the banquet hall, he'd thought about polishing off a whole bottle of champagne. He hadn't had but two glasses, hours before. Maybe some extra would have given him justification for what he wanted to do now. To step outside *everyone's* expectations. Especially hers.

He'd rejected the idea of more champagne, though. He'd never been much of a drinking man, and he wouldn't use liquor as an excuse for his behavior.

Besides, he didn't need alcohol to explain why he felt the way he did about Dana.

Glancing across the space between them again, he noted the way the pink lace of her dress lay across her shoulders. Then he forced his gaze to the road, where it belonged.

He had no right to look at her as she slept, unaware and vulnerable. No right to look at her at all. He was obligated to watch over her, to take care of her, as he'd promised his best friend he would do.

She'd made that damned hard for him.

He thought back to the day Paul had stopped by the ranch house on his last leave. The day Paul had asked him to watch over his family. Stunned by the request, Ben still had his wits about him enough to agree in an instant.

Paul and Dana and their kids were as close as family to him. He loved Lissa and P.J.—Paul Junior—as much as he loved his niece. He felt the same now about Stacey. Of course he would watch over them. All of them.

He had to keep that promise. Had to make sure he stayed close to Dana and the kids.

Staring at her with lust in his eyes probably wasn't the best way to get her to go along with that.

She woke up again just as they reached Signal Street, the town's main thoroughfare. He managed to smile at her briefly without making eye contact.

A few minutes later, after he'd turned onto her street and pulled into her driveway, he found himself grasping the steering wheel, as if his tight grip could rein him in, too. "Here we are," he said inanely, his voice croaking.

When he rounded the truck and opened the passenger door, she gathered her dress in both hands. Balanced on the edge of her seat, she hesitated.

The light from the streetlamp a few feet away turned her face pale as whipped cream and her hair buttery gold. Her eyes sparkled. He stood, one hand palm up, heart thumping out of rhythm, the way he'd waited after he had invited her to dance.

Finally, she reached out to him. Though he'd had the heater on low for the ride home, her fingers felt cool. Automatically, he sandwiched her hand between his. "You should have said something," he reproached her. "I'd have cranked up the heat."

"It's okay." She slipped free and walked toward the house.

For a long moment, he watched the pink-skirted sway of her hips. Then he came to his senses. As she unlocked the front door, he caught up to stand beside her.

"Coffee?" she murmured.

Not such a good idea. He forced a laugh. "You're not awake enough to make coffee."

"Of course I am," she shot back.

He'd said just the wrong thing. Or had he? Had his subconscious picked just the *right* words to guarantee she would argue the point?

She frowned and pushed the door open. "It will take more than the ride home to settle me down after all the excitement today. And it's the least I can offer to say thank you."

You could offer me something else.

Fingers now curled tight around a nonexistent steering wheel, he followed her into the house and the living room he'd once known so well.

"Have a seat," she said. "I'll be back soon."

Obediently, he dropped onto her couch and sat back as if he didn't have a care in the world.

Yeah. Sure. At least he'd gotten the obedient part right. No one in town would have cause to argue with him about that. Not even Dana.

He knew what folks thought of him—he'd lived with the knowledge his entire life. Good old Ben Sawyer. Well-behaved, safe, trustworthy Ben. Ben, the boy-next-door. All compliments, all good qualities to have.

The trouble was, not one of them appealed to him now.

The moment Dana went through the doorway into the kitchen, he sat up. He needed to pull himself together. To get control.

Not much chance of that, all things considered. Since grade school, he'd struggled to get a handle on the crush he had on her. Struggled—and failed. Years ago, that calf-love had turned into a powerful longing. And tonight, holding her in his arms had shot all his good intentions to pieces.

No matter how long or how hard he fought, he would never win.

Because no matter how wrong it made him, he wanted his best friend's wife.

Chapter Three

Leaving Ben as quickly as her pink high heels could carry her, Dana escaped to the kitchen, seeking safety in her favorite room in the house. But once there, she felt the walls closing in. As a tenant, she couldn't make permanent changes, but she'd decorated with blue-and-white towels and curtains to match her dishes. The normally soothing colors did nothing for her now.

Throughout the room, she'd hung so many houseplants Lissa often said they ate their meals in a garden. *A jungle,* five-year-old P.J. insisted every time.

An appropriate description at the moment, as she roamed the room like a tiger on the prowl, too tense to sit while the coffee brewed. Too aware of Ben just a few yards away.

After the dance, the ride home in the car and the sight of him sitting comfortably on her couch, nothing could calm her. And she had to go back into the living room and make polite conversation with him—at this hour! Why hadn't she said goodbye at the door instead of inviting him in?

Not wanting to admit the answer to that, she gathered mugs and napkins and turned the teakettle on.

Ben would only want coffee, though. She knew that about him and a lot more. His coffee preference: black, no sugar. His favorite food: tacos. Favorite cookie: chocolate chip. Favorite ice cream: butter pecan. What she *didn't* know about Ben Sawyer wouldn't fill the coffee mug she'd set on the counter.

What he didn't know about her...

She stared at the teakettle, which took its sweet time coming to a boil. Maybe better for her if it never did. Then she wouldn't have to go into the other room and face the danger of getting too close to him and the disappointment of knowing all the things she wished for could never come true.

This reprieve in the kitchen couldn't last much longer. Unfortunately. She had to stop obsessing about Ben.

She had to think of her kids. And her husband.

The reminder froze her in place.

Not all that long ago, her marriage had become about as solid as the steam building up in the teakettle. She and Paul had both known it, but before the issues between them could boil over, he announced he had enlisted. No warning. No compromise. No discussion. She'd barely had time to adjust to the news when he'd left for boot camp.

She had tried to see his decision as a positive change, a chance for him to come home a different man. For them to work things out. She owed her kids that. But the changes didn't happen for the better. His letters slowed to a trickle and then stopped arriving altogether.

When he came home on leave, the brief reunion was more uncomfortable than happy. Their final time together, she'd made one last attempt to save their relationship— an attempt that had failed. By the end of his leave, they'd agreed to a divorce. And to keep that between them until he returned after his discharge.

Only, he hadn't returned at all.

She'd been left with kids she loved more than life, a load of debt she might never crawl out from under, and renewed determination to hold on to the truth. A truth she had sworn no one—especially Ben Sawyer—would ever learn. A determination that Ben, so full of kindness and concern, undermined with almost his every breath.

Beside her, the teakettle screeched and spewed steam. *Like a dragon,* P.J. always said.

She looked at it and shook her head. Dragon or no, the kettle didn't scare her. Neither would Ben.

As long as she didn't get too close to either of them.

With an exasperated sigh, she moved across to the coffeemaker and poured a full, steaming mug. She was stalling, delaying the moment she'd have to face him again, whether he scared her or not. Quickly she poured her tea. Then she stiffened her spine and stalked toward the doorway to the living room. There, she faltered and stood looking into the room.

Tall and broad and long limbed, he seemed to take up much more than his share of the couch. He had left his jacket in the truck. While she had gone to the kitchen, he'd undone his tie and the top few buttons on his shirt. The sight of that bothered her somehow. Maybe because he hadn't hesitated to unwind, yet she remained strung tight.

He turned his head her way. His dark eyes shone in the lamplight. A smile suddenly curved his lips.

"I made myself comfortable," he said.

"So I see." Obviously he felt right at home, while she felt…things she definitely shouldn't allow herself to feel.

"You haven't changed much."

Startled, she stared at him. Then she saw he hadn't meant her at all. His gaze roamed the room, scrutinizing the well-worn plaid fabric on the couch and chairs, the long scratch on the coffee table where P.J. had ridden his first tricycle into it. Ben had been there that Christmas afternoon. He had bought that tricycle. Was he thinking about that now, too?

· Nothing in the house had changed since he'd last vis-

ited. But she had. "No, not much different in here," she answered with care, as if he would pick up on the distinction.

With equal care, she handed him his coffee. For a moment his fingers covered hers. She nearly lost her grip. The
hot, dark liquid sloshed dangerously close to the point of
no return. When he took the mug, pulling his fingers away,
she gave a sigh of relief mixed with regret.

Still, she hesitated.

She glanced across the room at her rocking chair, so
nice and far from the couch. But with such sharp edges on
the rockers, ready to pierce the lace of her dress. She'd lost
even that small chance of escape.

One of P.J.'s dinosaurs sat wedged between the couch
cushions. She plucked it free and dropped it on the coffee
table. Then, cradling her tea mug, she took a seat.

"Your hands still need warming?" he asked.

Again she stared. If she said yes, would he take her hand
between his again, the way he had when she'd climbed from
his truck? Her palms tingled at the thought. But of course
he hadn't meant that as an offer. How desperate must she
be, wanting his attention so badly she found it where none
existed? At least, that kind of attention?

She shook her head to clear it as much as to answer his
question.

From under her lashes she watched him set the mug
down on his thigh, holding it in a secure grip, as if he
didn't want to risk spilling coffee on her old couch. Or on
his tuxedo pants.

He had large hands with long, strong fingers, firm to the
touch from all the hours—all the years—he'd spent working
with them. No town boy, Ben Sawyer. He'd always lived on
his family's large ranch on the outskirts of Flagman's Folly.

Working with real estate, she knew to the acre how much
land Ben Sawyer owned. Not as much as Caleb Cantrell

now did, but a good deal more than most of the ranchers around here. She knew to the penny the worth of Ben's land, too.

Not as much as his worth as a man. Or as a friend.

She took a sip of her tea, understanding she was stalling again. She could list Ben's good points forever, but now she used them to keep her mind occupied so her mouth couldn't get her into trouble.

"How's the ranch?" she asked finally. A safe subject.

"Still there, which says something in this economy. You haven't come out since we raised the new barn."

So much for safe. "Work has kept me busy."

"I'm sure. Well, I'll need to have another potluck one of these days, before the weather turns."

Again she wondered if his words held a hidden meaning. No. Not Ben. But she couldn't be quite as open with him. Since Paul's death, she'd made it a point of visiting Ben's ranch with the kids only when he had a potluck. When there would be plenty of folks there. And even then she felt uneasy. Unable to trust her judgment around him.

Just as she felt now.

"We've got a couple of new ponies the right size for Lissa and P.J."

Her laugh sounded strangled. "Please don't tell them, or I'll never get Lissa to stay home and focus on her homework."

"Is she struggling with it?"

"Some. Mostly math. I try to help her, but a lot of it's over my head. It's gotten tougher since we were in school."

"A lot of things have." He sounded bitter. He smiled as if to offset the tone. "I can stop by and give her a hand."

Oh, no. She had to nip that bad idea before it could blossom into another problem. "Thanks, but she started going for tutoring. With Nate. I think they're catching on."

"Good." But he sounded disappointed.

Refusing to look at his face, she stared down at her tea. She couldn't risk having him come around here, getting close to the kids again. Sending her emotions into overdrive every time she saw him.

"Well." He gestured to the coffee mug. "What happened to my cookies?"

She looked up at him in stunned surprise. That was no casual question, was it? That was a direct quote of his own words, something he'd once said to her time and time again, beginning with the first week of her eighth-grade cooking class.

He sipped from the mug.

His averted gaze gave him away, proving he'd asked that last question deliberately. He'd meant to remind her.

Hadn't he?

Yet, truthfully, everything he said and did, everything he was, only made her recall their long history.

Everything she thought and felt only made things worse.

"Sorry," she said. "I'm all out of cookies."

"That's no way to say thanks for a ride home, is it?"

"If I'm remembering correctly—" she paused, cleared her throat "—I offered coffee, not dessert."

"A man can dream, can't he?" Now, over the rim of his mug, his eyes met hers.

Her heart skipped a beat. He couldn't be flirting with her. Not Ben. He couldn't want more.

Even though she did.

"Sure," she said finally. "Dream on." She looked down at her mug and blew lightly on the inch of lukewarm tea that remained, pretending to cool it. Needing to cool herself down. Needing to get him out of here—before she gave in to her own imaginings and made a fool of herself. Her cheeks burning, she added, "Speaking of dreams, I...I guess it's time for me to turn in. And for you to go. Before it gets too late."

"It already is."

She stared at him.

He shrugged. "It's nearly one o'clock, and I'm usually up by four. It doesn't seem worth it even to go to sleep, does it?"

"Not for you, maybe. But I intend to get a few hours in before I pick up the kids."

He nodded. "I'd better go, then."

Relief flowed through her. Two minutes more, and she'd be safe. She set her mug on the coffee table and rose from the couch. She had turned away, eager to lead him to the door, when he rested his hand on her arm. She froze.

"Before I go," he murmured, "you might need some help."

"I don't think so. I can manage a couple of mugs."

"That's not what I meant." He tapped her shoulder lightly. "Did you plan on sleeping in this dress?"

"No," she said, hating the fact that her voice sounded so breathless. That she *felt* so breathless. She must have imagined his fingertip just grazing her skin. "I thought Lissa would be here."

"She's not."

"I know."

She swallowed hard. Why had she ever wanted to make a dress she couldn't get out of herself? Why did she not regret the decision now? She could have saved herself some heartache.

She turned to him, and their eyes met. Unable to read his—unwilling to let him see what she knew he'd find in hers—she spun away again. "Well, you can unbutton the top two buttons. That ought to get me started."

Behind her, he laughed softly. He touched the low-cut

edge of the back of her gown. Her breath caught. As he undid the top button, his knuckles brushed the newly exposed skin. She clutched her lace overskirt with both hands and hoped he had touched her deliberately.

He undid the second button, his fingers following the same path along her spine. Warmth prickled her skin.

When he reached for the next button and the next, she closed her eyes, wishing he'd meant to set off the heat building inside her.

After he'd undone the back of her gown, she turned, already planning the quick farewell that would send him on his way. With one look at him, her words disappeared before they reached her lips. Now she could read his eyes clearly. Could read naked longing in his face.

A longing she recognized too well.

In those endless months when she'd known in her heart her marriage to Paul was over, she had begun to yearn again for all the things she had always wanted in her life. All the things she had hoped Paul would be but never had been.

A solid, steady, dependable partner.

A husband she could truly love.

A daddy who would willingly raise her children.

A man…

A man just like Ben.

"Think I've gone far enough?" His voice rumbled through her. No sign of laughter now. His chest rose and fell with his deep breath. He looked into her eyes, then let his gaze drift down to her mouth.

She had spent the entire evening wanting him to kiss her—and she couldn't wait for him to kiss her now.

Slowly he reached up and rested his warm hand flat against the back of her neck. She tilted her chin up, let him cradle her head in his palm, allowed her eyelids to drift closed.

His breath fanned her cheek.

The brush of his lips against hers came with the lightest of pressure. Not tentative, but restrained, as if he touched her in awe and disbelief. That sense of reverence made her eyes sting. Made her heart swell.

He cupped her face, his fingers curving beneath her jaw, fingertips settling against her neck. He couldn't miss her rapid pulse.

His head close to hers, he murmured, "You know, I've had a crush on you since kindergarten."

"No."

"Yes. Although I admit," he added, his voice hoarse, "I didn't think about this until a few years later." He slid his hand from her neck and wrapped his arms around her, holding her close.

When she opened her eyes, she found his face mere inches away. "You're only looking for cookies," she teased.

"Oh, no. Not when I've just had something much better." His mouth met hers again. "You taste like wedding cake."

She smiled. "You taste like champagne."

"Only the best for you, darlin'. Always."

Always. The way he'd been there for her.

Yet through all the years she had known him, she'd never imagined they would ever kiss. During the recent months when she'd begun to dream about him, she'd never dared to let those dreams bring her this far.

She had to clear her throat before she could speak again. Still, her voice cracked. "Are you trying to sweet-talk me, cowboy?"

"*Sweet?* No, ma'am." He shook his head. "I'm thinking more like hot." He slid his hand into the unbuttoned back of her gown, pressing his fingers wide and firm against her. The soft material slipped from her shoulders.

Not breaking eye contact with her, he trailed both hands

down her arms. Like the water bubbling in the country club's fountain, the gown fell in a froth of pink satin and lace.

When he took her hand and sank onto the couch, she went with him, wanting to get even closer, to brace herself against his solidness, to absorb his warmth. Wanting to hold on to a reality she wasn't yet sure she believed.

A few minutes later, though, she believed in him with all her heart. Despite his words, he was gentle and kind and sweet. And yes…later…he was hot, too.

He gave her everything she'd ever dreamed of. And more.

An even longer while later, she reached up to slide her hands behind his neck and link her fingers against him. As she held on, unmoving, he explored once again, running his hands down her sides, cupping her hips and holding her closer.

When she sucked in a deep breath, one side of his mouth curled in a smile. "This isn't what I expected when I drove you home tonight."

"That makes two of us." Like a schoolgirl, she struggled to hold back a giggle of pure joy at being two halves of a couple with him.

"And," he said, "this isn't what I expected when I promised to take care of you. But you don't hear me complaining."

Her throat tightened, and the giggle died. "No," she said, "I don't." Goose bumps rippled along her skin.

To accompany the chill running down her spine.

"In fact—"

"Wait," she interrupted, meeting his eyes. "You said 'take care'?"

He nodded. "Of you *and* the kids."

She tried to keep her tone even, her voice soft. "And you made that promise to…?"

He shifted, as if the question she'd left hanging caused him considerable discomfort. A small gap opened between them, and her body cooled.

"To Paul," he said.

"I see." She sat up, needing more distance between them. When he let her go, she grabbed her gown from the floor and slid into it, heedless now of the fine lace, of the delicate satin. "That's the reason behind everything?" she asked. "Because you made a promise to Paul?"

He leaned against the arm of the couch. "What 'everything'? You mean us, here?"

"We've never been 'us, here' before tonight." She wouldn't—couldn't—think about that now. It took twice as much effort to keep her voice level as it had to stifle that foolish giggle. "No, I mean everything you've done. Trying to help me. Stopping by my office unannounced. Buying the office building. All that—because of what you promised Paul?"

Frowning, he nodded. "Yeah. But I'd have done those things anyway. Why wouldn't I? I told you, you've been the girl for me since kindergarten."

"How long ago did you have to make that promise?"

"The day he shipped out at the end of his leave. But there was no 'have to' about it. I willingly gave him my word."

"I'm *not* willing to let you take care of me."

"It's too late for that."

She frowned. "Why?"

"I've watched over you for years. Ever since we were kids in school."

"Then it has to stop. We're not kids anymore. And as I've told you before, many times, I can take care of myself—and my children. I don't think you'll ever understand that." She tugged the bodice of her gown into place. "And I think it's time for you to go."

For a few long moments he didn't move. Then, slowly, he curled his fingers into fists and stared at her, his eyes narrowed.

She had no fear. This was Ben. He was good and kind and meant well. And because he was so good and kind, because he felt so determined to take care of her, she'd hurt him.

After he'd just made love to her as if—

She couldn't finish that thought. She couldn't sit here and watch him walk out.

Instead, she rose from the couch, then crossed the room. "Good night," she said over her shoulder. Her voice shook.

"Running away won't help anything," he said.

"I'm not running," she answered, climbing the stairs without looking back. Without stopping. "I'm just standing on my own."

On legs no steadier than her voice had been and that threatened to give way at any moment.

From the upstairs hallway she listened to his movements below.

When he left, she went down again to lock the door.

Then she sank onto the rocking chair. Her heart thudded painfully. She had wanted to stop him. Wanted to call him back. But she couldn't. She had to make him leave, had to force him to understand she didn't need him.

She had to force herself to accept a painful truth, too. For all this time, Ben had considered her his responsibility.

She couldn't allow that to continue.

No matter what she had heard for years from another man, no matter what that man had tried to make her believe, she wasn't anyone's burden. Never had been—and as long as she lived, never would be.

Especially not Ben's.

Chapter Four

Dana dropped Stacey off at the day care center, then drove toward the elementary school. She needed the Monday-morning routine after spending most of Sunday agonizing over Ben. Again and again, she'd replayed what had happened between them.

Cheeks flaming, she glanced in the rearview mirror at Lissa and P.J. She needed to think about her children, not Ben.

Taking a deep breath, she looked at the kids again. Thought of her routine.

Of course, when she needed a distraction more than ever before, her office would be quieter than usual with Tess, her sole employee, away on her honeymoon. That meant she'd have plenty of time alone. Plenty of time to obsess over Saturday night—and then to forget it had happened.

But how could she ever forget anything about Ben when everywhere she looked, she saw reminders of him? Even the squat, redbrick school building and the bus pulled over in the parking lot brought back memories.

Years ago, Ben and the younger kids from the outlying ranches only came into town when they rode the bus to school in the morning. As soon as the final bell rang, they immediately rode the bus home. With their parents busy working, the kids didn't get to hang out in Flagman's Folly until they could drive themselves back and forth.

Ranch families had the same problem today. She and Kayla Robertson already had a plan in the works, one Ben would eventually hear about thanks to his seat on the town council. She dreaded having to face him the night they would present their proposal.

"Mom, stop," Lissa shouted from the backseat. "There's Nate." In the rearview mirror, Dana saw her point off to one side of the schoolyard, where her best friend had just jumped down from Tess and Caleb's SUV.

Dana blinked in surprise at seeing Tess in the driver's seat. The newlyweds had spent a couple of days in Santa Fe but were scheduled to leave that afternoon for a cruise. She unbuckled her seat belt and climbed out of the van with the kids.

The two girls walked away, chattering and hiking their backpacks up on their shoulders. Carrying his lunch box and scuffling his feet, P.J. trailed behind them, unwilling as always to have anyone see him arrive with the girls.

Dana shook her head, then turned to Tess. "What are you doing here? Isn't your ship sailing?"

"Yes, but we have plenty of time before our flight for the coast. We decided to come back and surprise Nate and Mom at breakfast before Nate left for school."

Relieved, Dana nodded, unable to hold back a smile. "On Saturday, you said Nate was the one dealing with separation anxiety. But you're the one missing her already, aren't you?"

Tess shrugged. "It's silly, but you're right. I've never been away from her before."

"It's not a bit silly. I'd feel the same way." Happy to have something to keep her mind—and Tess's—off Ben, she said, "She'll be all right. Your mom and Ellamae will keep a close eye on her. She's got plenty to keep her busy.

And Lissa can't stop talking about the sleepover in a couple of weeks."

"I know, Nate reminded me about it three times on the way over here this morning. Well, I'd better get going. I left Caleb back at the Whistlestop, making a few last business calls before we head out. Dana…"

At Tess's hesitant tone, she frowned. "What?"

"He's not happy leaving before the closing on the ranch."

Dana stiffened, sure she knew where Tess was going with the conversation. A former bull-riding champion turned ranch owner, Caleb Cantrell had invested his money wisely and had plenty to spare. He also now had a wife and daughter to spend it on.

Dana felt Tess's happiness as if it were her own.

Which meant she could also understand her friend's worry for her. She worried, too. For the sake of her children, she had to find a way to lighten her own load. A permanent solution. The commission from the sale to Caleb would definitely feed her hungry checkbook. But that money was just one more thing in her life…like love and marriage… that wouldn't last forever.

Hoping she sounded unconcerned, she laughed and shook her head. "You two need to stop worrying over everyone else and go enjoy your trip. Tell Caleb I'll survive till you get back."

"It wasn't only your survival he was thinking about. He's eager to get his hands on that ranch."

"He should be focused on getting his hands on his new wife."

Tess laughed. "We're taking care of that. Oh, before I forget, he wanted me to tell *you* something. A friend from his rodeo days is going to get in touch to look at property. His name's Jared Hall."

"Great."

Tess nodded. "But really, Dana, Caleb said he'd cut an advance check on the commission—"

"Enough. Quit trying to mother me." She smiled to soften the words. "I'm not Nate. But like her, I'll be all right until you're home again. Now, just stop. And," she said, faking a threatening tone, "if you *don't,* you're fired."

"Okay, okay. I definitely want my job. By the way, did you have a pleasant ride home with Ben the other night?"

She couldn't help flinching at the change of subject. Or more truthfully, at the mention of his name. She forced herself to meet Tess's eyes and raise her brows in mock-surprise. "'Pleasant'? You've never used that word in your life. Of course we had a 'pleasant' ride. What else would you expect?"

"Since you've asked…the two of you have seemed awfully uncomfortable with each other lately."

"We're fine."

"Maybe you are, at that," Tess said, her face suddenly as blank as P.J.'s when he was caught up to mischief. "I admit, you looked pretty relaxed in his arms on the dance floor the other night." As Dana opened her mouth, Tess raised her hands palms out and grinned. "I'm not asking anything about it. I'm just saying…whatever's going on with you two—"

"There is nothing going on. And I can handle our landlord. Very *pleasantly,* too."

Tess laughed and gave her a quick hug. They said their goodbyes, and Tess waved as she drove out of the parking lot.

Dana climbed into the van and slumped back against the driver's seat. No one else watched her. She was trying— and failing—to hide from herself.

How could she have lied like that, and to her own best friend? She *couldn't* handle their landlord. She couldn't deal

with her emotions about him at all. Worse, she couldn't believe where those emotions had led her. And the risk they
had caused her to take.

Everyone in town made it plain they would always consider her Paul's wife. They would always worship Paul.
Only two days ago she had worried about their reaction to
seeing her dance with Ben at the reception.

What would folks say now, if they knew the widow of
their beloved army hero had slept with his best friend?

BEN LOOPED Firebrand's reins around one of the posts of
Sam Robertson's corral. The stallion's dark chestnut coat
gleamed in the setting sun, giving credence to his name.
Ben patted the horse's flank. As if in resignation, Firebrand
snorted and nodded his head. Then he stood and stared over
the corral rail.

Squinting against the sun, Ben waved to Becky, out near
the barn with her puppy. Sam's little girl waved back. Pirate
yipped a couple of times, then settled down at her feet again.

Seeing Becky and her dog led him to think of P.J.

That took his mind straight to P.J.'s mama. No surprise
at the leap—or at what followed. Guilty thoughts flew in
his brain like the flies buzzing around Firebrand's twitch-
ing tail.

Sam came out of the house carrying two long-necked
bottles. "Here. Have a seat."

Ben nodded his thanks and took his time swallowing
some of the ice-cold beer. It felt good going down.

It felt good to sit on the picnic bench in Sam's yard and
watch the sun sink. He'd spent the past few days working
hard, and he needed a break from the ranch. He needed a
break from himself.

No matter how much he'd tried to keep busy with work,

he couldn't stop himself from going over what had happened at Dana's house just a few days ago.

What the hell kind of friend would make a move on his best friend's wife?

"She's got a few new tricks, too," Sam said.

Ben started. "What?"

Sam chuckled. "Man, your mind must be a thousand miles away from here."

No, just taken a ride into town.

"I was telling you about Becky and Pirate," Sam said. "She's taught that pup some more tricks."

"Good." He nodded. "Good for kids to have a dog."

"Yeah. I just said that." Sam looked him in the eye. "Obvious enough you didn't catch a word of it. What's the trouble?"

He shrugged. "No trouble. I'm unwinding." He gestured to the catalog Sam had dropped onto the picnic table. "Is that the breeder's article you wanted to show me?"

Sam nodded, and the talk turned technical, lasting the length of their first beers and requiring a backup.

When Sam suggested a third, Ben shook his head. "That's enough for me. I've got to get back to the house and check on that new mare."

"Have you talked to Dana this week?"

"No." He picked at the label on his beer bottle. "Was there a reason for me to?"

"No idea. Kayla mentioned you at suppertime. She's going into town to see Dana tomorrow, and I guess the office put the thought of you into her head. You don't need to do much there, though, do you? Besides collect the rent."

"There are things that need some attention. But all in all, it pretty much takes care of itself."

"Sounds like you made a good investment, then. I wish the ranches could run themselves, too."

"No, you don't. We've got to do something to earn a living."

They laughed at that, but later, as he headed homeward on Firebrand, he thought of the comment again. And of Dana and the tough time she was having.

There had to be something he could do to help her. Some way to keep in touch with her—without *touching* her. A way to take care of her without ticking her off.

If that could ever be possible again.

Through the years, guilt over his feelings for her had grown like the wild, choking kudzu that would take over his spread if he and his cowhands didn't keep a handle on it. The prettiest flowers you'd ever want to see, that kudzu. But deadly to the stock that grazed on his land.

And now with that load of guilt increased ten times over, it just might be the end of him, too.

Dammit, but he should have known better. Trying not to think of the other night, he took Firebrand into a gallop. His thoughts caught up with him anyway.

Dana had looked so beautiful in that pink dress. And—for the first time in his life—he'd found her within his reach.

He couldn't keep from touching her, couldn't help but want to get her out of that gown and into his arms. Couldn't stop himself from making love with her.

For the only time in his life?

He leaned into Firebrand, urging him to fly as if a monster nipped at their heels.

EARLY FRIDAY MORNING, Dana sat at her desk at Wright Place Realty. Outside the storefront window, Signal Street was bathed in September sunshine. Inside the office, she felt swathed in a sense of gloom heavy enough to cut with a knife. She missed having Tess around. She missed seeing Ben—though that was the last thing she should want.

Thank heaven, Kayla had shown up for their meeting, giving her a much-needed break from her wayward thoughts. She leaned back in her swivel chair and looked across the desk. "This idea's sounding better and better every time we discuss it."

Kayla smiled in satisfaction. "I know it is."

They wanted to convince the town council to build a playground for the children of Flagman's Folly, a place where kids of all ages could come together. At the moment, the town's limited options included the day care center, with its small fenced-in area, and the sneaker-worn plot of grass running behind the elementary and high schools.

"We've got some time till the next council meeting," she told Kayla, "but we need to start looking for locations. First, though, we should check zoning ordinances."

"I can take care of that. You might have your hands full with Ben."

She stiffened. "Ben?"

"Yes. He told Sam last night he's thinking about doing some work in here."

She tried not to groan. When he had bought this building, he had promptly lowered her rental fees. If he planned to sink money into the property, would he feel the need to raise the rent again? Would he do that regardless, as a way to get back at her for what had happened between them?

No, not Ben.

Still, by the time the newlyweds returned, she could be in big trouble. Maybe she should have agreed to Caleb's offer of an advance. But accepting, after the way she'd denied needing it, was out of the question—even though Tess had probably seen right through her. After all, they had both been in the same precarious financial situation until just recently. Well, fingers crossed, Caleb's friend Jared would prove himself a real, live customer.

Avoiding Kayla's eyes, she straightened the paperwork on her desk. "I'm sure, sooner or later, I'll hear what he's got in mind."

"I'd go with sooner." Kayla sounded amused. "He's just about to walk in the door."

"WHAT CAN I DO FOR YOU today?" Dana asked.

Seeing her through the office window had cranked up the heat inside Ben. But now he winced as a chill settled over him. One that had nothing to do with the air that swept into the room as Kayla pulled the door closed on her way out.

Come to think of it, she'd left in a hurry. Maybe she hadn't much cared for the chill around there, either.

Behind her desk, Dana looked cool all over, too, from her blond hair to her blue blouse to the bare hands she had folded in front of her. A big difference from the way he'd seen her last, with her hair loose and her pink dress unbuttoned and her pale skin peeking through the back of the gown as she'd run up the stairs. She had just sent him on his way and, still, it had taken everything in him to keep from following her.

He tightened his grip on the clipboard in his hands and swallowed hard. *Steady, now. Just friends.*

Her icy question, one she would've aimed at anyone who walked through the door, said she might not even consider them that. "Uh. Listen, about the other night—"

She turned red to her hairline. "Please." She coughed and began again. "That's…something we shouldn't mention. Forget the other night. I have."

He nodded. She'd forced her tone to go along with the whole cool package, telling him she had no intention of making things easy between them. Well, he'd already taken on that job. To make things better. Not to argue with her but to help her.

Whether she wanted his help or not.

Of course, with the way she felt about that, he couldn't tell her outright. He raised his hand, waving with the clipboard he held. "I need to take a few measurements."

"What for?"

Her question took him aback—until he saw the small indentation between her brows. After all these years, he could read her every expression. The tiny frown meant something worried her. Keeping his tone level, he said, "I'm thinking about putting down new tile in here."

"There's nothing wrong with the floor."

"An upgrade might be nice, don't you think?"

She shrugged. "If you want the truth, I think it's fine the way it is."

Why had he bothered to ask? "Thanks for the input." As nicely as he could, he added, "Think I'll go with the new tile. Might look good to your customers."

She sighed. "We don't have any clients, Ben."

He stilled. That sentence told him what had caused the worry line between her brows. Hearing it took the irritation right out of him. The sudden wry smile she sent his way made his pulse jump.

"You know, if Caleb hadn't bought that ranch," she added, "I'd be up Sidewinder Creek without a paddle."

"We've done that once before, haven't we?"

She laughed. "Yes, I guess we have."

Their eyes met. For a moment the shared memory from their grade-school days brought them close again.

"And," she continued, "you'd think I would learn from my mistakes."

She meant more than that day long ago. "Well," he said, unwilling to go where that would lead, "the thought of getting caught right now can't be so alarming, considering the creek's about a foot and a half deep from the drought."

"You know what I mean."

"Then all the more reason to try to lure customers for you."

She stared at him. The close moment ended as abruptly as if she had slammed the office door between them. "Thanks," she said finally. "But I can manage."

"How?" he asked, gripping the clipboard. "You're not expecting another Caleb Cantrell to just happen along, are you?"

"Maybe. A friend of his is flying in next week to look at property. But—"

"Yeah, Caleb mentioned that."

"—my business isn't your worry."

"Fair enough." No, it wasn't fair at all. Her words stung, and he fought to shrug off his frustration. "This office *is* my concern, though. So is the entire building. And if I see improvements needing to be done, I'll make 'em."

"Fine. As long as you're aware I'm not obligated to pay you anything more than the rent we decided on. And that was no gentleman's agreement we made."

"Couldn't have been, since I'm no gentleman." He gave a rueful smile. "Neither were you, last time I looked."

No matter the chilly tone she'd forced earlier, no matter the blank expression on her face now, he could start a campfire with the tension sparking between them. He could start something more.

Give them time alone again—

"We have a lease," she said, her voice shaky. "Signed and sealed on the dotted line."

"I'm not arguing that."

"Good." She rose, marched across the office and flipped

the hanging sign on the front door. From the outside, it would now display Closed.

She must have read his mind.

"Well, then," she said, "as there's nothing else to discuss, I'll leave you to get your measuring done."

Disappointment jolted him. "No need for you to go."

"Oh, but there is. I've got customers to lure in, and all that. Please lock up on your way out." Clearly all too eager to get away, she went through the door and closed it behind her even more quickly than Kayla had done.

He slapped the clipboard against his palm and shook his head. What the hell had he been thinking, wanting to get her alone? Hadn't that led to enough trouble?

So much for his plan of working around here—every time he would come in to do something, she'd just take off again. He couldn't ask her to stay at her desk, anyway, when her job required her to keep on the move. But he wasn't beaten yet.

She didn't know what a mistake she'd made by walking out on him. By forcing his hand. By making him twice as determined to find a way to make things easier for her.

He smiled, turning another idea over in his mind, one he liked much better than hoping to corner her in her office.

An idea he'd stake his ranch on she wouldn't like at all.

"I DIDN'T DO IT, MAMA!" P.J. called the minute she walked in the door late that afternoon.

Now what?

After Ben had invaded her office, seeming to take up all the oxygen in the room, she'd found it hard to breathe. Needing to go somewhere—*anywhere*—to escape, she'd spent a long morning researching at the local library. Then she'd spent an even longer afternoon back at her desk, searching for listings, hoping to find something to tempt Caleb's friend next week. Yet somehow, as she worked, she could still see Ben in the room.

Coming home to P.J.'s vehement denial gave her an instant diversion. Chances were, he *had* done whatever it was. She just hoped it wasn't something too serious.

"Didn't do what, P.J.?" she asked.

Instead of answering, he took her by the hand and led her to the downstairs bathroom.

Water trickled from beneath the vanity. Puddles saturated the tiles. The loose edges of a half-dozen vinyl squares had already started to curl. She groaned. "P.J., where's Anne?"

Dana couldn't ask for a better babysitter. She willingly picked up P.J. after kindergarten and nine-month-old Stacey from day care. And she was always available in the evening when Dana had to show properties to her clients.

When she had clients.

Best of all, Anne loved the kids. And that mattered most.

"She's in the backyard with Stacey," P.J. said.

Chances were almost guaranteed that Clarice, her elderly next-door neighbor, would have her eye on the yard, too. "You go out there with them, please, while Mama cleans up this mess."

After walking barefoot through the rising water on the bathroom floor, she tied a rag around the leaking pipe and put an empty bucket beneath the joint. Finished, she looked around and shook her head. *This* was the floor—and not to mention, now the pipe—that should be replaced, not the perfectly good tiles Ben wanted to change in the office.

The floor and the plumbing headed a long list of things that needed fixing around here. She couldn't afford the repairs. At this point, she couldn't afford to move anywhere else, either. In any case, she didn't own this house, only rented it.

In the kitchen, she grabbed the phone and punched her absentee landlord's number. Despite numerous reminders about repairs, she'd let George slide, knowing he had his own financial worries. She tried to ignore the issues, but her list had grown to a couple of pages, the minor fixes had given way to major problems, and this new situation threatened her family's safety.

She would never ignore that.

Frustrated at getting George's answering machine, as usual, she left a short but specific message. If she didn't hear from him by the end of the day, she would pack up and move out.

As if.

She'd just finished mopping up the last traces of water when the phone rang. *George, already?* Maybe miracles did happen.

And maybe, if she'd gotten tougher with him from the beginning, the miracles would have occurred sooner, and the minor fixes wouldn't have become major issues.

But it wasn't George returning her call.

Instead, she heard Kayla's voice. "Dana, my sister's flying in next Saturday. Sam and I want to surprise Becky. His mom has plans. Could we leave her with you until we get home?"

"Of course. Lissa has the girls here that weekend, and—"

The doorbell rang. *Another chance at a miracle?*

"This might be my landlord. I'll talk to you again, but definitely plan to bring Becky here that day."

She ended the call and hurried to the front of the house. But when she threw open the door, the man standing there was not George.

"Ben?" She couldn't stop the thrill that shot through her at seeing him on the doorstep. His gaze moved over her shoulder to the living room, where the couch sat just a few

short yards away. Gripping the doorknob, she fought to keep herself and her tone steady. "What are you doing here?"

Like five-year-old P.J., he could be a man of few words when the situation warranted it. He simply held up a toolbox and a roll of duct tape. Then he moved past her and headed down the hall. She closed the door and followed slowly, feeling no less confused.

In the bathroom, he was on his knees in front of the sink, with his broad shoulders inside the vanity as he assessed the leak. *She* assessed the well-worn jeans pulling taut all over. After a good look, she croaked, "How did you know about the plumbing?"

"George called me." His voice sounded muffled.

Well, of course. The obvious answer, if only she'd paused to think. But somehow, thinking and analyzing and acting rationally had gone out the window lately. At least, every time she found herself in Ben's company. The formfitting jeans didn't help. Still, she could focus enough to know that something here didn't add up. "Why in the world would George call you?" she demanded. "Why didn't he come here himself?"

"He's out celebrating."

That response made no sense at all. "Celebrating what?" As if it mattered.

"Freedom from foreclosure." He'd deliberately deepened his voice, making the words ring hollowly in the enclosed space. He backed out from beneath the vanity, sat on his boot heels and looked at her. "I've taken a huge load off George's mind."

"How?" Unable to look at him, she moved her gaze to the sink. Turning on the faucet wouldn't be a good idea right now, but her throat desperately needed water.

"You're a real estate agent," he said. "Can't you figure it out?"

Of course she could. She already had. *Believing* the awful idea was something else. "You bought out George's loan?"

"I sure did." He grinned. "As of this morning, I'm the owner of this house."

Chapter Five

Dana parked her van in front of the house and waited while the girls in the backseat gathered their belongings.

"Don't forget your overnight bag," Lissa said to Nate.

Dana glanced toward the garage and Ben's dusty, dented ranch truck. Sighing, she shook her head. In the week since his shocking announcement, he'd nearly become a fixture in her home.

No, that word didn't fit. *Fixtures* stayed still and remained quiet and made life better for people, not worse. Nothing on that list of features came anywhere near to describing Ben's impact on her life. He'd done nothing but upset her routines, her thoughts, her balance.

In short, he'd upset *her*.

"Hey, I know that truck," Nate said. "Ben's here?"

"He's here *every* day," Lissa informed her in a tone Dana couldn't quite read.

"Cool."

Not so cool, in her opinion. Not when reality forced her to face the *true* reason for her upset.

Every afternoon she longed for a reprieve from dealing with Ben. And with every arrival home she caught herself in the lie. Because the sight of his truck outside the garage never failed to excite her.

Still, she stared at that dusty pickup truck in despair.

What was wrong with her? She was a grown woman. A mother with small children. She had put behind her all the memories of…that incident with Ben.

Yet she showed every sign of a schoolgirl with her first crush. Relief. Elation. The heart-pounding attack of nerves that came with knowing she would soon see "him" again.

The girls tumbled out of the van, backpacks slung over their shoulders. Nate carried her overnight bag, too.

Anne came out of the house holding Stacey. From the open doorway, P.J. took one look at the girls running in his direction and went back inside. As Lissa and Nate raced into the house, Dana started more slowly up the path.

Anne met her halfway and handed Stacey to her. "All yours. I've got to get going."

After kissing the baby's fair hair, she looked at her sitter in surprise. "I usually have to pry you away from the kids to send you home. Everything all right?"

The teen's cheeks turned bright red. "Got a date," she mumbled. "With Billy. From Harley's."

Dana smiled in understanding. Billy was a tall, blond forward on the high school basketball team. From what she'd seen on her trips to Harley's General Store, where he worked after school, he was in demand. "Very nice, Anne. You'll have all the girls in Flagman's Folly envious tonight."

She giggled. "It's our first date," she confided. "We're going to the early show."

"Well, have fun. Be careful. And I'll see you on Monday."

"Okay." Anne chucked Stacey under her chubby chin, grabbed her bag from the porch step and took off down the sidewalk.

Watching her go, Dana cradled the baby against her and sighed. What she wouldn't give to be that young and innocent again. That hopeful.

Or would she?

She'd had her own man-in-demand, and look where it had gotten her. Her infatuation with Paul had disappeared a long time ago. Along with her love for him.

Stacey squirmed in her arms, and guilt flooded through her. Paul had given her three wonderful children. For that alone, she owed him more than she could ever have repaid.

"You planning on staying out here all night?"

She turned back to the house to find her new landlord standing in the doorway. He wore a pair of scuffed cowboy boots, threadbare jeans and…a smile.

This was good old Ben? It had to be, but she needed to look him over one more time, just to make sure. Her gaze got hung up somewhere between his belt buckle and his chin, lingering on his flat belly, taut chest and tight nipples. That night with him, she'd touched every bit of that goodness.

Her palms itched for the pleasure again.

She forced her gaze upward, reaching his mouth. His smile had disappeared. His eyes looked wary, yet they suddenly glittered. He was recalling that night, too.

She hadn't realized she'd held her breath until she exhaled in a rush. The blast ruffled Stacey's hair. Her daughter giggled. The sound broke whatever spell had transfixed Dana.

No matter what had happened between them such a short time ago, he was *still* good old Ben. For heaven's sake, she'd seen him in swim trunks every summer of her life. Well, at least until a few summers ago. He had seriously buffed up since then.

Or else her memory was going.

"Actually," she said, finally getting to his question, "I would like to go inside, if you don't mind."

"That can be arranged." Stepping back into the house, he held the door open for her and Stacey.

That was the trouble with Ben. He was always too willing to arrange anything he thought she wanted. Reluctantly, she climbed the steps and moved past him, trying not to inhale as the scent of his aftershave wafted toward her. Trying to ignore the sound of his footsteps as he followed her into the living room.

She set Stacey onto her blanket on the floor. The baby immediately grabbed her favorite teething ring.

"You're home late," Ben said.

She turned to him and felt relieved to note he had put on the blue T-shirt she'd seen hanging on the stairway banister. "Realtors work all kinds of hours," she told him. "I don't punch a time clock."

"Anne must have forgotten that." He dropped into her rocking chair. "I didn't think she'd make it till you got home. She was about to wear a trench into the front walkway, with all her pacing up and down."

She straightened one edge of the baby's blanket. "Anne was eager to go get ready for a date. I didn't know that or I'd have tried to get home sooner. We stopped to pick up a guest. As you've probably figured out."

"Nate?"

"Nate. She's staying with us for the weekend." She pushed the box of P.J.'s dinosaurs into the corner beside the couch. "They've got more friends coming later tonight and sleeping over till Sunday, too. Things will be hectic around here. Which reminds me…" She paused, trying to find the right words.

He raised one brow as if in question.

"I appreciate all you've done these past few days," she said finally. Truthfully. Every improvement to the house and yard only made things better and safer for her children.

But she'd have to speak carefully now, so as not to give herself away. "I understand you want to fix up your property. But can't you do the repairs during the day, when I'm—" she grit her teeth and tried again "—when the kids aren't here underfoot?"

Now both brows shot up. "Not hardly. I've got a ranch to take care of, too."

It was that little word *too* that pushed her past the limit. "You *are* busy, aren't you? First a ranch, then an office building, and now this house and a family, as well."

"Family?" He looked puzzled. "You mean, your kids?"

"Yes, mine." She sank to the couch and pulled the afghan over her lap in a vain attempt to protect herself from her own emotion. "Ben, I know you have only our best interests at heart, and I know you want to help. To keep your promise." Her breath caught. She couldn't think about that. "But it's not necessary. Though I thank you for wanting to try," she added hastily, seeing the look on his face.

She didn't want to hurt him. She just wanted him to leave her alone to do what she had to do. As if she'd spoken the thought aloud, he rose from the rocking chair. She bit her tongue, not wanting to give him any reason to change his mind.

Finally, he nodded. "You're right."

She had braced for a farewell argument. His response made her sag against the couch in surprise. And relief. Thank goodness, at least she wouldn't have to worry about *him* underfoot this weekend. As it was, she would have enough to do trying to keep P.J. happy in a houseful of females.

"I *am* busy with the ranch," Ben admitted. "That takes priority."

"Absolutely," she agreed.

"But not tomorrow. I'll be back in the morning. Bright and early."

"Ben—"

"Look. This has nothing to do with helping you. Do you want to see my deed for this place? It's signed and sealed on the dotted line."

She winced, recognizing the words she'd said to him that afternoon in her office. The afternoon he'd bought her house. "All right." She gave in—since she didn't have a choice. "What time should I expect you?"

"We start at sunup out on the ranch."

She stared at him for a long moment, then got up to spread the afghan over the back of the couch. When she'd taken enough time to make it clear she didn't plan to respond to his ridiculous statement, he said goodbye and left.

She plopped back onto the couch and looked at Stacey.

Her daughter took the teething ring from her mouth and made a noise that sounded like "Pffftth."

"My thoughts exactly, sweetie."

Resting her head back against the cushion, she closed her eyes and thought again of what she and Ben had done on this couch.

The memory alone left her breathless. But other memories, much older and much sadder, made her chest tighten and her eyelids prickle with tears she refused to shed.

Long ago, she'd made the mistake of falling for the wrong man. One who had eventually taken her love for him and turned it to his advantage. Who had tricked her into believing she needed him and couldn't survive without him. He'd laid his trap and snared her. But she wouldn't ever let herself get caught again.

Not even by Ben Sawyer, a good man. The best man. A man who, in his own way, caused her more trouble and heartache than Paul had ever done.

Ben was laying a trap for her, too. One baited with kindness and concern, with kisses that made her heart melt, and caresses that made her pulse pound, and words she yearned to believe.

A trap more dangerous than the first one because she found it so tempting.

BEN HAD MENTIONED SUNUP only as a way of getting a rise out of Dana. When she didn't jump down his throat, he'd felt oddly disappointed. Somehow, having her snap at him seemed a whole lot better than that long, silent look she'd given him. A look that said she thought he was out of his mind.

While he didn't actually intend to show up at the crack of dawn, he found himself ready long before nine o'clock the next morning, with everything that needed doing already done. He didn't mind the work, because he loved this ranch. He enjoyed going through the routines his daddy and granddad had once taught him. Still, long years of practice meant he could finish up quickly.

Now he paced the floor in the ranch house kitchen much the way Dana's babysitter had paced in front of the house last night.

Considering Anne had expected Dana home by then, he'd grown concerned about her absence, too. That old van of hers had broken down more than once in the past year or so. And she was so independent, so sure she could handle everything on her own. He'd be damned if he'd let her get away with that.

He couldn't.

He couldn't stay away from her, either.

After grabbing his keys from the counter, he headed out to the hall. There, he paused only long enough to yank on his boots and pluck his Stetson from its hook on the coat stand.

Eager to get to town, he made the short trip in record time.

As he stood on Dana's front porch and rang the bell, a sense of discomfort washed over him. Not from tension. Not from guilt. From something he couldn't find a name for. Maybe he didn't want to identify it. He'd already felt too many things this week since buying Dana's rented house out from under her.

But, whatever else he didn't know, he felt certain of that decision.

The front door opened. Paul Wright, Jr., stood on the doorstep staring up at him. He'd known P.J. since birth. Yet as often as he'd played catch and checkers and cards with the boy, he'd never seen him just the way he was right now—looking the spitting image of the five-year-old friend Ben remembered.

The sight took him aback. The thought that came right on top of it took his concerns about his own actions away. How did Dana handle seeing her husband in P.J. every day?

The boy gave a huge yawn and rubbed his eyes with his fists. "I didn't sleep last night, Ben," he announced, walking away.

Ben shut the door behind them. "Why is that?" he asked, though he could have hazarded a fairly accurate guess.

"Girls."

P.J.'s opinion of the fairer sex matched the way Ben felt about cattle rustlers. "It must be tough on you, being the only man in the house."

"Yeah. Not like when my daddy was here. But he went to the army, and now he's not coming back anymore."

He sucked in a deep breath. He'd talked often enough

with Dana's kids about their daddy, but never about his death.

He sure hadn't given much thought to Paul, either, when he'd held Dana in his arms the night of the wedding. Maybe that explained the discomfort he'd felt while standing on the doorstep.

"Yes, I know," he said finally. "Your daddy won't come back." But, lately, he'd felt as though Paul had never left.

P.J. climbed onto the couch, pushed aside a blanket covered with pictures of brightly colored dinosaurs and flopped back against a small mountain of pillows. Evidently, he had spent the night in the living room.

"And now," the boy said, yawning again and closing his eyes, "there are all these *girls* around here."

"Maybe they won't stay long."

P.J. opened one eye briefly. "*Ha.* They'll be here till *tomorrow.*"

An awfully long time, from a little boy's perspective. Not that short in Ben's view, either. Last night, *tomorrow* had seemed very far away.

So had Dana and her kids.

He shook his head. He had to stop these kinds of thoughts. They'd bring him nothing but trouble. Maybe they already had.

P.J. lay with his mouth open, snoring gently. Smiling, Ben leaned down and settled the blanket over him. Finished, he turned toward the kitchen. And found Dana standing in the doorway, watching him.

He returned her scrutiny, taking in the pair of denim shorts that stopped way up on her long legs, her Flagman's Folly High School T-shirt, and the hair she'd pulled into a ponytail.

"While you're at it," she said, "don't forget to check out the dark circles under my eyes."

"What dark circles?"

"*Ha*—as P.J. would say." She turned back toward the kitchen.

He followed her through the room and out the door onto the back porch. "So you heard our conversation."

"Yes." She leaned over to pluck something out of a laundry basket, and those shorts rose even higher on her legs.

He felt like rubbing his eyes the way her son had. Glad for the reminder, he said, "What does P.J. know about Paul's death?"

"What you heard." She shook out a small towel and hung it on the clothesline strung from the porch rail. "It's enough for him now, at his age. I'm not sure he remembers a lot about his daddy. He wasn't even four yet the last time Paul was home."

"And Lissa?"

"Lissa knows more." She jabbed at the line with a clothespin. "She remembers a lot more, too."

"She misses him?"

"Of course she does."

The question seemed to surprise her. He'd bet the next one would leave her stunned. He asked it anyway. "What about you?"

She froze. The bedsheet she held up momentarily hid her face. Then she lowered the sheet and he saw her eyes again.

Dark circles or none, it didn't matter. She'd always had beautiful blue eyes.

"Ben, we've been friends all our lives," she said slowly. "But that's not a question you should be asking me."

"Why not? I'm trying to get a handle on your thoughts, since you're unwilling to come right out and tell me. You said it yourself, we're friends. What's wrong with acting like one?"

"That's just it," she burst out. "It seems like you're always acting with me. And then the night of the wedding, one minute we're friends, and the next we're—" She stopped short, her cheeks reddening. She clutched a damp towel against her. "Never mind. That night was just as much my fault as yours. But you—" Her voice broke. "I can't understand you anymore. I don't know what happened to the friend Paul and I grew up with."

He was the one left stunned now.

She shook out the towel. "Look, it's probably just me. It's been a long night, and I got even less sleep than P.J. did. Let's just forget what I said and agree to another truce, okay?" She gave him a crooked smile. "Don't you have some work to do around here? I know I do."

"Mama?"

At the unexpected voice, they both started. Lissa stood just inside the kitchen doorway. She wore pajamas and had her hair twisted into a handful of braids. Frowning, she looked from him to her mama.

"Stacey just woke up."

"Thanks, sweetie," Dana said. "I'll get her right now."

"Okay." Lissa stared at him for another moment, then left.

So did Dana.

Alone on the porch, he rested against the railing and looked out across her yard. She was right. He had been acting with her for a very long time. For the past year and more, as he tried to keep his promise to Paul. For nearly his whole life, while he hid his feelings for her. And now…

How could he blame her for not knowing what he was trying to do? He'd lost the answer to that himself when he'd gotten roped and tied by his own guilt.

Chapter Six

An hour later, when she heard Kayla greeting the girls in the backyard, Dana sighed in relief. "C'mon, sweetie." She gave Stacey a hug. "Let's go out to your swing."

Kayla stood in the yard, still talking with the girls. Becky had already joined them at the picnic table. Though the five-year-old was much younger, Lissa and the rest of the girls got along well with her. Surprisingly, P.J. did, too. He especially enjoyed her visits when she brought her lively little puppy along.

Today, she'd come without Pirate. Still, her arrival might help him settle down and accept that he needed to be nice to Lissa and the other girls.

She hoped Kayla's arrival might help *her* settle down, too.

After her uneasy conversation with Ben earlier, he had gone upstairs. As he worked in Lissa's bedroom, directly over the kitchen, every squeak of a floorboard made her hold her breath, waiting for his step on the stairs. Every pound of his hammer reassured her she didn't need to worry. For that moment.

On the shady back porch, she strapped the baby into the swing, wound the crank and gave the seat a gentle push. Stacey waved her arms and giggled.

P.J. sat on the top step. He gestured toward the potted plants and gardening tools that took up one end of the porch. "Mama," he said, "there's no place for my dinosaurs to walk."

"I know, sweetie," she said. Most of the plants should have been hung, but she hadn't found time to put up the hooks she'd bought. "I'll make space for them one day soon."

Earlier she had seen him keeping watch on Lissa and her friends, who had gathered at the picnic table. Now that Becky had arrived, he looked almost with longing at the group. "Why don't you go and sit with them? Becky will be happy to see you."

He shook his head. "Nah. I don't wanna play with girls."

"Oh." She smiled. Now wasn't the time to explain that Becky fell into that dreaded category. As she went down the steps, she ruffled his hair.

Kayla had crossed the yard to talk to Dana's next-door neighbor, Clarice, and Tess's aunt Ellamae.

Dana joined them. "Good morning, ladies."

"A loud morning, too," Clarice said.

Her tone surprised Dana. Clarice never minded the kids' play in the yard. And truthfully, the girls hadn't made much noise at all after coming outside this morning. Then her neighbor's gaze drifted to the second floor of Dana's house. The sound of hammering rang through the open bedroom window.

"Ben's here," Ellamae stated.

Dana nodded.

"He's been here quite often lately," Clarice said.

"Stands to reason, doesn't it, since he bought the house?" Ellamae asked. Not waiting for an answer, she sent Dana a sideways glance and added, "He'd help out whether he owned the place or not. In fact, I reckon he's volunteered a time or three before now. That's just his way."

At this obvious attempt to fish for information, Dana clamped her jaw tight. But for a second, doubt assailed her. Ellamae always knew everything. Maybe she was hinting at something. But she couldn't know what had happened here the other night.

There was no use arguing over the older woman's assumption about Ben. Her good opinion of him would never change. Besides, she only said what everyone else in town thought.

"Gotta hand it to him," Ellamae went on. "Ben Sawyer's always been such a good, steady boy. A good thing he bought the house, too. No offense, Dana, but I'll bet there's plenty needs fixing up. That lazy George would let the place fall to ruin. Of course Ben will take care of things over there."

Of course. That was the problem. No one in Flagman's Folly thought twice about Ben helping her. In fact, they expected it. She shivered, thinking of what they would all say if they ever suspected what had happened between the two of them.

"Ben is a *very good* friend to Dana," Clarice said. "He was like a brother to Paul. And you couldn't find a better man than Paul. My Vernon always said so. Rest both their souls…" A loud buzzer almost drowned out her hushed words. When the noise stopped, she said in a normal tone, "Well, that's the dryer." She hurried away.

"Before I forget," Ellamae said, "Roselynn wants y'all to come over tomorrow to welcome the newlyweds home. Two o'clock. Nothing fancy, just burgers. Kayla, you'll tell Sam?"

"Sure. Roselynn mentioned it the other day."

Ellamae turned to her. "You and the kids'll come?"

"Of course."

"Good. I'll leave it to you to extend the invitation to

Ben—seeing as he's here more than he's home lately." Ellamae nodded and headed toward Clarice's back door.

Dana bit her tongue. She should have realized Ben would
be included in the invitation. But she couldn't back out now.

She and Kayla walked over to stand near the porch. Overhead, Ben's hammering continued.

"Sounds to me like those ladies attempted to say something without coming right out with it." Kayla smiled. "And
I can make a good guess what that was. I don't know about
Clarice, but Ellamae, at least, wouldn't pass up a chance
to do some matchmaking—as Sam and I have good reason to know."

They did. So did Tess and Caleb and a few dozen other
couples Dana could name. But she shook her head. "Not
this time. Matchmaking would be the last thing on their
minds. That was their not-so-subtle reminder."

"Of what?"

"Of the fact Ben was my husband's best friend." As soon
as the words left her mouth, she wished she could call them
back. Kayla's puzzled expression only emphasized her need
to watch what she said. She waved at Stacey, happy in her
swing, then forced a laugh. "They just couldn't pass up an
opportunity to sing Ben's praises. That's a tune I've heard
all my life."

"Maybe he's worth singing over, if he puts all this effort into everything he does. Besides, you've been friends
forever, too, haven't you?"

"That's exactly what those two want me to remember."
The hammering ended abruptly, and her words sounded
loud in the sudden quiet. She lowered her voice. "And it
explains why they're so interested in what's going on over
here. I'll guarantee they're peeking through Clarice's curtains right now."

Kayla glanced over at the house and smothered a laugh. "You're right."

"I knew it." She sighed. "Kayla, you don't know what you walked into, moving to Flagman's Folly from the big city."

"I'm not sure I'd agree with that. We had our…interested neighbors in Chicago, too."

"Busybodies, you mean. Not like this. It's one of the biggest drawbacks of a small town. Your life is not your own."

"Actually, I love that." To Dana's relief, Kayla held out the plastic file folder she'd been holding and changed the subject. "Here are the copies of the ordinances. I'll leave them with you. Thanks again for keeping Becky while we go to the airport."

"My pleasure. She'll be happy playing with the girls till you get back." She took the folder and tucked it under her arm. "I'll look at this during the week. By then, we should be down to just a final read-through on the proposal. No worries, though—the idea's so perfect, the council won't be able to turn it down. The members will all vote yes the minute they hear about it."

"Is that so?"

She and Kayla both jumped at the sound of the deep voice booming from over their heads. Ben stared down at them from the porch, his hands braced on the railing in front of him.

"What is it we're going to be so all-fired excited about?"

Dana froze. She needed to remember to watch what she said around him, too. Especially around him. Naturally, as chairman of the town council, he would take an interest in any new proposals. "We're not ready to discuss it yet."

"Why not, if you already know which way the vote will go?"

Smiling, Kayla moved a step away. "Gotta run. I'll leave you two to sort this out. Sam and I need to pick up Lianne."

She crossed to the group at the picnic table. As she said goodbye to the girls, she signed her words to Becky.

The little girl answered, hands flying in the air.

Dana watched for a moment, smiling. Then, knowing she couldn't avoid Ben forever, she turned and trudged up the steps to the porch.

Arms crossed, he rested against the railing. He'd kept his T-shirt on—thank goodness!—but even through the fabric she could see the muscles of his chest and upper arms flex. *Good old Ben.* The reminder only made things worse. He didn't look a bit old—but he sure looked good.

She could look, couldn't she? Just as long as she didn't touch? As she waved goodbye to Kayla, her fingers trembled.

He glanced across the porch to where P.J. still sat on the top step playing with his toys. "Dinosaurs are fine," he said, his voice low enough that her son didn't hear. "But they're just toys. All kids ought to have a dog."

"Maybe." Shrugging, she glanced at P.J., too, then quickly away.

"Remember Buster Beagle?" Ben asked.

She had to laugh. "Of course. You know I *adored* him. I'd love to have another dog—someday. That just won't work for us right now. I wouldn't want the poor thing cooped up in the house when we're gone all day. And I can't see staking him to a tree in the yard, either." She frowned. "Besides, there are plenty of other things we need around here first."

Like school clothes. A washing machine to replace the one on its last legs. A nest egg to cover all the incidentals she and the kids needed. To pay off all the debts she owed.

Army survivor benefits only took her so far. And if not for Caleb's new ranch, the income from her real estate office wouldn't have taken her anywhere this year.

Ben looked out toward the picnic table. "With all the

girls around here," he said, his voice still low, "he could at least use a few other boys around."

P.J. pushed the cardboard box he used as his dinosaur "cave" closer to their side of the porch steps. To get within hearing distance of their conversation, she was sure.

"There aren't any boys his age close by," she said. "And it's hard for parents to set up playdates, especially when they don't live in town. I don't have to convince *you* of that." Why she also didn't want to share her plans, she didn't know...

All right, she knew very well. Once he'd heard about the project, he'd make it one more thing he wanted to help her with.

"It's easier over the summer," she added, "when the kids have more free time. Right, P.J.?"

He nodded, confirming her thought about listening in.

"He went for art classes the past couple of years." She smiled. "That's where we first met Becky and Kayla."

"Yeah, I recall that. Speaking of Kayla, don't you two want to start collecting votes for that proposal you're working on?"

He must have taken fishing lessons from Ellamae. She forced a smile. "Since your eavesdropping told you I'm so sure about the proposal, you must know I'm not worried about votes." Not meeting his gaze, she lifted Stacey from the swing. "You'll just have to wait till the next Town Hall meeting."

"If that's the way you want it." He sounded irritated. "Then I've got a proposal of my own."

She stiffened, her arms unconsciously tightening around the baby, who squirmed. "What are you talking about?"

"I *propose* to take a ride over to the Double S and pick up some tacos to feed this gang lunch."

"Thanks, but I—"

P.J.'s hand on her arm cut her off. He hauled himself to his feet. "Can I go with you? I can help you carry the tacos."

"Sure," Ben said. "Pick up your dinosaurs first, though. You wouldn't want them getting trampled."

"Okay!"

To her surprise, P.J. immediately began scooping the dinosaurs into their cave. He'd reacted with more enthusiasm than he ever showed when she asked him to straighten up his toys. Maybe the lunch menu had given him the incentive. He loved Manny's tacos, but with her need to watch her pennies so closely, they hadn't eaten out in a while.

Over his head, she met Ben's gaze again. Trying to ignore the sparkle in his dark eyes, she said, "I had lunch planned."

"Not enough for me, I'm sure."

None for you at all. But she couldn't say that with P.J. just inches away.

As it was, he looked up, his forehead wrinkled in concern. "We'll bring a taco home for Mama, too, right, Ben?"

"We sure will. *Two* for your mama," he promised. "After all," he continued, eyeing her as P.J. finished gathering his toys, "I'm working here through the afternoon. We might as well all eat together." He glanced down again. "C'mon, P.J., let's go see how many tacos the girls want."

"Okay." This time, her son took Ben's hand to haul himself to his feet. P.J. lowered his voice and confided, "I can count high. But don't tell the girls if I have to use my fingers."

"No problem, buddy," Ben said as they started across the sun-drenched yard. "Your secret's safe with me."

On the shadowed porch, Dana shivered. Ben's words rang in her head. She didn't want to think about secrets. At least, not her own. But his comment reminded her of the truth she'd kept from her family and friends all these years—the truth about her husband that no one, especially Ben, would ever accept. Because it wouldn't agree with their image of Paul.

Snuggling Stacey even closer, she breathed in the calming scents of baby powder, a laundered playsuit and just plain baby.

Over at the picnic table, Becky looked expectantly at Nate. The older girl raised her eyebrows and curved her hand into a claw, then ran her fingertips down her stomach. *"Hungry?"*

Becky bobbed her fist in the air emphatically. *"Yes!"*

Dana smiled. A shadow in Clarice's living room window caught her eye. The twitch of the curtain confirmed the two women still had her yard under surveillance.

Her smile slid away.

No matter what Kayla said, she couldn't really know what it felt like to live her entire life under a microscope. Dana did.

She loved her hometown and could never see herself leaving it. But even as a child, she'd realized there were things about growing up in Flagman's Folly she'd wished she'd had the power to change.

Such as knowing your past would always haunt you because no one would ever let you forget it.

"DANA WENT BACK INSIDE with Stacey," Clarice reported, peering around the edge of the window curtain. "Ben's out in the yard with P.J. and the girls. That man is wonderful with those children. But I'll tell you, Ellamae, he's spending a good deal of time over there. What will people think?"

To tell the truth, Ellamae didn't much care about anyone's opinion but her own. "We covered that, didn't we? He owns the house now. You ought to be happy. Considering all the work he's putting in, he'll raise the property values of the entire neighborhood."

"You think so?"

"Who mails out the town tax statements?" she asked, not expecting an answer. They both knew very well that *she* did.

"Ben's taking off in the truck now," Clarice said. "But he's got P.J. with him, so they'll be back again." She let the curtain fall into place and went over to her recliner.

"I'd like to know what those girls are up to," Ellamae said.

"Lissa and Nate?"

"No. Dana and Kayla. I heard Kayla came into Town Hall the other day to look up some zoning ordinances."

"What for?"

"I don't know." The admission bothered her. She liked keeping up with what went on in her town. "The judge and I were in court at the time, and nobody in the office asked her." That would never have happened if *she'd* been at the front desk that day.

And she would have asked Kayla outright when they'd all stood outside just a bit ago, if she hadn't been busy working on a more important plan. Or trying to, anyhow.

"I was talking with Kayla just before you pulled up," Clarice said. "She mentioned a proposal for the council."

Ellamae stared at her. "A proposal to do what?"

Clarice shrugged. "She didn't say."

Ellamae bit her tongue. The other woman did her best. Not like some folks who just didn't have a proper curiosity bone in their bodies at all.

As if she'd heard Ellamae's thoughts, Clarice said, "I'll see if I can find out from Dana."

"Good luck with that." Her own lack of progress still rankled. She cared for Dana almost as much as she did her own niece, Tess. One way or another, she'd find a way to get through to that girl. "When it comes to talking, she could give Ben competition. Except when there's something she doesn't want to discuss."

"She's got a hard life, raising those three children on her own. But she never says a word of complaint. Some people like to keep their troubles to themselves."

"Well, they shouldn't," Ellamae said flatly.

Clarice stared at her.

"I mean, they shouldn't be closemouthed with their friends." She ought to be more careful about what *she* said, though. Clarice didn't always understand what she was getting at. And worse, the other woman didn't always agree with her aims. "Talking over troubles is what friends are for."

"Maybe she's doing all her talking with Ben Sawyer now." Clarice shook her head. "I don't know. Maybe him stopping over there isn't so bad. They're friends, aren't they? They'll always have that connection, through Paul. And you know what my Vernon always said, rest his soul. You couldn't find a better man. And wasn't he right? Paul turned out to be a real hero."

"He did, didn't he?"

When Clarice picked up her knitting, Ellamae sat and brooded. Some of the woman's comments had caused her to reconsider her strategy.

"You know, Clarice," she said after a while, "I think on my way home later, I just might stop at Town Hall and look up a few ordinances myself."

"It's Saturday. Town Hall is closed."

Ellamae smiled. "Not to me it isn't."

Chapter Seven

Ben loaded his tools into the back of the pickup. "Almost done," he said to P.J. His half-pint helper had trailed him around all afternoon. "I've got just a few more things in the house."

"Don't forget this." With obvious reluctance, P.J. held out the plastic container of washers Ben had given him to carry.

"Hmm." He pretended to deliberate, then said, "Why don't you hang on to it? We'll need it next time I come by."

P.J. grinned. "Okay. I'll go put this on my dresser right now." He rushed away, not even hesitating when he passed the girls still gathered around the picnic table.

Ben followed more slowly.

As he approached Lissa, she looked at him. "Are you staying for supper?" she asked.

Her expression didn't tell him whether she wanted a yes or no. The thought made him realize that lately, for the first time, he'd had trouble reading Dana, too.

Before he could respond, Nate spoke up. "Of course not, Lissa. Ben's not here for the sleepover. Besides, he came to lunch. If he stays for supper, too, he'd just wear out his welcome. Right, Ben? That's what Aunt El always says."

He smiled. Funny how the two girls seemed to have ex-changed their mamas' personalities. Always the outspoken one, Nate took more after Dana, who'd never lacked for something to say.

Except recently.

He nodded at Nate. "You're right. Don't think I'll try pressing my luck tonight."

Still, as he turned toward the house again, he wondered what would happen if he hung around until Dana called the kids in to supper. She couldn't ignore him if he stood right there in front of her. Or could she? He recalled how she'd sidestepped the proposal question.

Worse, out in the yard at lunchtime, he could see how uncomfortable she'd felt around him. A few times, the conversation—and his heart—had lightened after she'd met his eyes. But for the most part, she had kept her gaze averted and had made sure the handful of kids stayed between them.

He entered the house and checked the first-floor rooms. All empty. He made his way upstairs and picked up his tools from Lissa's bedroom. The sound of Dana's voice coming from her own room drew him forward, tugging him as surely as if she'd thrown a lasso to pull him toward her.

Damned wishful thinking.

"I think we'll go have a—"

When he stopped in the doorway, she broke off whatever she planned to say to Stacey, who looked up at her from her walker. Mouth shut tight, Dana eyed him almost warily and eased back a step, stopping short against the bed he'd helped set up years ago. The bed he'd like to help her into right now.

Again, he damned himself. He'd already risked too much with her downstairs on the couch. How could he think of taking her here in the bedroom she once shared with Paul?

The baby smacked the rim of her walker with a plastic rattle. He knelt to chuck her under the chin, and she giggled. "I finished fixing the shelves in Lissa's room," he said.

"Thanks." Her gaze focused on the dresser, the open closet, the light switch on the wall. On anything but him.

Had she read *his* thoughts in his face? Probably not, or she'd have left the room. And still, he wanted to tumble her down on that bed. Rising, he shoved his hands into his back pockets. "I saw Ellamae leaving Clarice's earlier. She said you had a message for me."

Watching the baby, she said, "Roselynn invited folks over for tomorrow. To welcome Tess and Caleb home. Two o'clock."

"Sounds good. Want me to pick you and the kids up on my way over there?"

"That won't be necessary." At last, she looked at him, her brow wrinkled. "Why didn't Ellamae just tell you herself?"

He shrugged. "Maybe she was in a hurry to get home. Does it matter?"

"I don't know. But have you ever known her *not* to have some motive for anything she does?"

Her question reminded him of her claim that he acted with her. He acted now, pretending this conversation could distract him from the thoughts going through his mind.

She picked up the baby. "I'm going to put Stacey in for a nap." She walked around him and out of the room, leaving him standing there staring at that big empty bed.

After a minute, he shook his head and turned to leave.

Lissa stood in the hallway, her frown a match to Dana's and suspicion written all over her face. "What are you doing?"

"Talking with your mama."

Her eyes widened. She leaned into the room to inspect it. "There's nobody in here."

"I know—"

"Lissa?" Dana called. "Are you looking for me?"

"Yes," she answered, but she still stared at him.

Dana appeared in the doorway. "Ben? I thought you'd left. I guess we'll see you tomorrow at the Whistlestop."

So much for an invitation to supper. "Yeah, you sure will."

She and Lissa stepped back from the doorway, and he took his leave. As he went down the hall, he could feel their gazes boring into his back.

Nate had hit it right. He'd outworn his welcome here.

DANA CROSSED TO HER DRESSER and began brushing her hair. Faintly, she heard the front door close downstairs.

"Ben's here a lot now, isn't he?" Lissa asked.

Dana turned. Lissa had always been her quiet child, so unlike P.J. She very seldom talked about anything that bothered her. Both the look on her face when she'd stood staring at Ben and her hesitant question now made Dana's stomach twist.

She couldn't let her feelings for Ben jeopardize her children's relationship with him.

"Why does he have to be here?" Lissa demanded suddenly.

Choosing her words with care, she replied, "Well…he bought this house, and he needs to make a lot of repairs."

"Why? George never fixed anything."

"He did, once in a while. But Ben is eager to get things done."

And that was another thing about Ben Sawyer. His take-charge attitude. A wonderful quality for a man to have—and Ellamae hadn't lied about George. He didn't have it. Neither had Paul. She just wished Ben didn't feel the need to take charge with her.

Lissa frowned. "Nothing ever went wrong in our house when Daddy was here."

"Sweetie, that's not true. Lots of things needed to be

done around here, but your daddy didn't always have the… the time."

"Ben sure does."

She nodded. "Yes. He makes the time and goes out of his way to help other people."

"He always helped Daddy, too."

She gripped her brush more tightly. "That's right, he always did."

"But Daddy's gone and he's not coming back. Why does Ben still have to come here?"

She swallowed her surprised gasp. "I told you, he owns our house now. Besides, even though he has work to do here, he likes to have the chance to come and see you and P.J. and Stacey."

"I don't care. I don't want to see him."

How could she tell Lissa that she didn't want to see him, either? She couldn't. Instead, she said softly, "I know it's hard for you to have Ben over when your daddy's not here anymore. But Ben would be very sad if he couldn't come and see you."

"Then how come he hasn't been here all along?"

"Because he lives on his ranch. You know that. We've visited there many times." But that wasn't what her daughter meant, and she knew it.

"He's not like Daddy," Lissa said. "He didn't go into the army. And he's not like Nate's daddy, either. Caleb was gone being a rodeo star. Ben didn't go anywhere."

"Of course not. He has to take care of his ranch." Although it didn't seem like that lately. She forced a smile. "That's enough talk for now. I think we'd better get downstairs to your guests, don't you?"

Lissa left the room.

She followed, one hand pressed to her stomach, as if that could ease the weight in the pit of it.

The talk with Lissa had only made her feel worse. Every response she gave her daughter reminded her of yet another of Ben's many good qualities.

And of something more.

Once, she had worried herself sick over how little Paul did with their children, how infrequently he even bothered to talk to them. Ben had treated the kids so much better— and had spent more time with them.

All these months she had avoided him, all the days she'd made excuses to prevent him from stopping by the house, she hadn't realized just how much his absence had affected her children. Until now.

P.J. had latched on to him as if afraid he would disappear from their lives again. Lissa had once trailed at Ben's heels, too. And now he'd become a stranger to her; she didn't want him around.

All because Dana had acted out of desperation, trying to save herself from heartache.

A heartache she hadn't managed to escape, after all.

DANA SHIFTED ON THE PICNIC bench in the crowded backyard of the Whistlestop Inn. Most of the townsfolk had showed up to celebrate the return of the happy newlyweds.

The party had started in midafternoon, and the sun now drifted toward the horizon like a worn-out birthday balloon. Still, everyone lingered. Most of the adults had gathered at one end of the yard, while the children played games at the other end. As usual, the women had settled at the picnic tables nearest to the house so they could keep an eye on replenishing food and drinks.

Almost against her will, Dana had found herself keeping an eye on Ben.

Now, even as she tried hard to focus on Tess's story about the honeymoon cruise, part of her attention wandered a few tables away to where Ben sat with Ellamae's boss, Judge Baylor.

The two men had settled in with a couple of mugs of lemonade and a bowl of chips. They seemed less interested in the food, though, than in what they were discussing. Their gazes occasionally shifted to the tables where the women sat.

More than once, Ben's eyes had met hers. Each time, she looked away hurriedly, yet she couldn't help wondering what he was thinking. Couldn't help wishing she could turn into a fly and land on their table to listen to their conversation. Or maybe even better, manage to fly away from here altogether.

Too restless to sit still, she jumped up from the bench. "I'll go in and get some more lemonade." She hurried toward the house. Just as she finished refilling the pitcher, the kitchen door opened.

Tess slipped into the room. "Finally!" she exclaimed. "I've waited all day for a few minutes alone with you." She sank into a chair and grabbed a handful of paper napkins. "My excuse for coming inside. Sit a minute. Fill me in. What have I missed?"

Dana took a seat. "Not a lot. Though, thanks to Caleb, the best news is we've lined up a possible new client."

"Yes, he told me Jared's flying in Tuesday. He'll stay with us here. We've got plenty of vacant rooms, unfortunately. But at least that'll keep him handy." Tess laughed. "I can just imagine what Nate and Lissa will say once they hear we have another rodeo star living in Flagman's Folly."

"If we find something to suit him."

"We will. I'll be in early tomorrow to get started."

"You're *that* eager to leave your new husband?"

"Well…actually, he needs to go to Montana for a couple of days. Some trouble with his ranch foreman up there.

Believe it or not, though, I *am* ready to get to work again. And it's so nice to be home."

"And to see everyone, I'm sure. Especially Nate."

"That, too. You were right—she survived fine without me. I hear she had a great time at your house with the girls." She raised her brows. "I also hear they weren't the *only* ones spending time with you."

Dana tried not to sigh. Of course Tess would have found out immediately. "I suppose you mean Ben buying the house."

"I do. What a surprise. Mom and Aunt El couldn't wait to *share the news.*"

Despite the situation with her new landlord, Dana responded with the second half of their inside joke. *"Of course not,"* she said, managing to keep a straight face until Tess rolled her eyes. Then they both burst into laughter.

"Anyhow," Tess continued, "I know George wasn't the greatest landlord, and he certainly didn't keep up with all the house repairs. You must be so glad to have Ben there."

Glad? If she only knew...

The kitchen door opened, and Ellamae peered from around the edge of it. "You girls planning to stay in here all afternoon? We've got thirsty people outside waiting for that lemonade."

"Coming right up," Dana said, grabbing the pitcher again. The interruption couldn't have come at a better time—because she couldn't have come up with a decent response to Tess's comment if they *had* sat at this table all afternoon.

Her best friend would never understand why she didn't want to have Ben around. No one would, unless she told the truth about Paul. And she couldn't do that.

Without a word, she followed Tess and Ellamae outside.

A couple of the men had joined the group of women at their picnic tables. Not Ben, though.

No matter how she tried to stop herself, she immediately found herself seeking him again.

Before she could glance away, he turned his head in her direction. For a long moment, she *couldn't* look away. Like a scene from a movie, everything around her—the conversation, the laughter, the movement—all seemed to stop. As if, for just that moment, only the two of them stood in the yard.

Which was ridiculous.

She forced herself to turn toward the nearest table. Hands shaking, she grabbed a paper cup and filled it with lemonade. As she sipped the drink, she glanced around her. No one seemed to have noticed anything. Yet again, she gave in to the urge to look in Ben's direction. He now sat leaning forward, listening to Judge Baylor.

Could she have imagined that frozen moment?

Fortunately, she didn't have time to think about it.

"Over here, Dana," Ellamae called. "Bring that pitcher."

Happy to oblige, she chose a seat across from Tess and Caleb, putting her back to Ben and the judge.

At the next table, Kayla sat with her sister, Lianne. With their long, honey-blond hair and blue eyes, they could have passed for twins. Like her little niece, Becky, Lianne was deaf. Unlike Becky, she used her voice and could read lips when people faced her directly as they spoke to her.

At the moment, Lianne was carrying on a conversation with Becky, Lissa and Nate, who had just slid onto the vacant bench at their table.

Caleb had draped his arm around Tess, and she leaned into him, her face the picture of contentment. Dana's heart swelled at the sight of her friend's happiness.

"So, Caleb," Ellamae said, "you decide yet what you're doing with that new property you're buying?"

"Running it as a working ranch, for one thing, raising cattle. Maybe some horses."

"Rodeo horses!" Lissa said eagerly, speaking like a true rodeo fan.

"And then we can come out and ride them!" Nate said. "Right, Becky?" She put her thumbs against her temples with the first two fingers of either hand extended. *"Horses!"*

Becky laughed and fluttered her upright hands in the air. *"Yay!"*

Tess laughed, too. "Gee, I wonder where this little once-upon-a-time city girl caught the horse bug?"

From hanging around with Nate, Lissa and the other girls, of course, who had all long ago been bitten by the rodeo bug.

"That's an idea," Caleb told the girls, smiling at them. "A ranch can always use more horses."

"How about a dude ranch?" Kayla asked. "You could bring in vacationers from the city, too."

Ellamae, Clarice and a few of the other older women told her what they thought of that—nothing at all.

"City folks who come to stay are one thing," Ellamae said. "Dudes are something else."

"I have an idea," Lianne said. "What about a kids' camp?"

Caleb's brows shot up. He turned so she could see his face. "Not a bad suggestion, Lianne."

Other folks at the table nodded agreement.

"That's not the only good idea around here this afternoon," Ellamae announced. "Dana, we've been talking about you. Or rather, reckon I should say we were talking about Paul."

Dana had just topped off a cup of lemonade for the woman next to her. For a moment, she froze with the pitcher in midair.

"Yes," said Clarice, "we think it's high time folks in town did something to honor him."

"Sounds good," Caleb said. "What do you have in mind?"

"Not sure yet," Ellamae said. "We've just started planning it. We're thinking of setting up a statue in his memory."

Dana wrapped her hands around her cup and stared down at the pulp swirling in the lemonade. Her insides felt as though they were swirling, too. She desperately needed a drink but didn't feel sure she could swallow.

"We'll need to get folks on board," Ellamae continued. "Talk up the idea, do some fundraising."

"Count me in."

Startled, she gripped her cup so tightly, it threatened to buckle. Ben had spoken from directly behind her. Having the women talk about her husband was bad enough. Having him add his two cents was almost more than she could bear.

"Isn't it, Dana?"

He had moved to stand at the end of the picnic table near her. She shifted on the bench, hoping to hide her reaction from everyone. "What?"

"I said the statue, or whatever the group decides on, is no more than Paul deserves."

"You're right there," said Ellamae, directing attention her way again.

As the conversation continued, Dana slowly let out the breath she'd been holding and gave silent thanks to the older woman for saving her from another awkward situation. From having to respond when she had no clue what to say.

She had no idea how to handle her reaction whenever Ben came near her, either. The past year and more had already strained her nerves. The past couple of weeks had stretched them almost to the point of snapping. Here at the Whistlestop, at her office, and, worst of all, now even in her home, her frequent contact with him only made it harder for her to forget.

To forget what they'd done that night after the wedding.

To forget Paul, the best friend Ben had lost, the boy and later the man everyone in Flagman's Folly had looked up to. Paul, the husband she had stopped loving long before he had died.

She lived with that knowledge daily. She didn't need any reminders. And she certainly didn't want a statue—a solid, unmovable, *permanent* reminder—of memories she longed to forget.

From the end of the table, Ben frowned and watched her.

With a shaking hand, she raised her cup to her lips and took a cautious sip. Though she managed to swallow, the lemonade didn't do a thing to steady her. It didn't help calm her racing thoughts at all. It didn't give her a single solution.

How could it, when she had no way out of her dilemma?

Sometimes, she dreamed about telling folks the truth. About what Paul was like. About how he had treated her. But for her children's sake, she couldn't. For Ben's sake, she wouldn't. She was well and truly trapped, stuck forever in a web of deceit.

A web she had spun herself.

BEN DOWNED ANOTHER MOUTHFUL of lemonade. The tart flavor on his tongue almost hid the bitter taste Dana's reaction had left in him a while earlier.

Almost.

Across the picnic bench from him, Caleb said, "The statue for Paul sounds like a great idea."

Ben agreed. Too bad Dana didn't see it that way. "He deserves all the accolades we can give him."

"You're right," Caleb said emphatically, looking shaken.

Ben well understood that. Though Caleb had grown up in

Flagman's Folly, he hadn't been around when they'd learned of the tragedy of Paul's death. He'd only found out on his return to town.

Folks here still hadn't gotten over the shock. No wonder Caleb looked upset. "You knew about his decision to join up?" he asked now.

"Yeah, he told me ahead of time. That's a day I'll never forget."

Because the announcement had come as a complete surprise.

"You get to talk to him after he enlisted?"

"Yeah. A few times. He came home one last time, too. He'd seen a lot of action, things he didn't want to talk about. You know Paul, though. He took on the role of soldier the way he did everything else." With determination and the desire to excel and an almost uncanny belief that nothing would get in his way. To that point, nothing had. "You should've seen all his medals."

They'd met up several times in that brief trip Paul had made home, and Ben was pleased when Paul stopped by the ranch again on his way out of town. That visit added one more entry…one final entry…to his store of memories of his best friend.

He'd been different that last time, edgy, uptight and distracted. Eager to get back to action, or so Ben had figured. Impatient to return to his new life or not, something had riled him up that day. He couldn't have known he would never see Flagman's Folly again.

Or, maybe he'd had a premonition of some kind, telling him he would never return.

Whatever he'd had on his mind, Ben suspected it had triggered the recollections Paul shared that day. Had prodded him to remind Ben about their past, to reinforce their long friendship. To talk about the bond between them.

A soldier, Paul said, needed to be able to rely on his platoon, to trust the men who had his back.

The way he trusted Ben.

That's when he had asked Ben to watch over his family, speaking with an intensity that gave his request the weight of a solemn oath. With the same determination Paul had shown all through his life, Ben took that oath, knowing he would let nothing get in his way. He had never anticipated having to carry it out.

And then...

"Tess told me how it happened," Caleb said. "About the evacuation."

"Yeah. They got the women and kids out of the village, saved them all."

And then Paul's platoon was ambushed. In the chaos that followed, Paul dragged one of the downed soldiers to safety. Yet he hadn't been able to dodge a bullet himself.

In an instant, his best friend was gone.

"Paul died a hero," he said flatly.

And Ben had been left to fulfill his oath.

He could never break the promise he'd made. Never betray his best friend's trust. Yet, hadn't he done that, after all?

Hadn't making love with Dana been the ultimate betrayal?

If nothing else would force him to keep his hands off his best friend's widow, that would.

His best friend's widow...

Again, his stomach churned at the sourness of the lemonade he'd swallowed, mixed with the remembrance of Dana's reaction earlier. She didn't like the idea of a tribute to her husband. He couldn't understand it.

How could she *not* want to honor Paul?

Chapter Eight

"I don't know, El," Roselynn said, frowning as she loaded glasses into the dishwasher. "You might be wrong this time."

Ellamae looked sharply at her sister. The last of the guests had just left the Whistlestop, and they were alone in the kitchen.

"Wrong about what?" Ellamae demanded.

"The statue for Paul."

She glared. "When we talked about it last night, you thought it was a fine idea."

"And I still do. It's a wonderful honor for him. But I'm not sure what we should do about Dana. The poor girl looked like she didn't know which way to turn when you brought it up this afternoon."

Tess walked into the room with a load of serving trays. "Almost done," she said.

She didn't always care for what her aunt and mama got up to. Ellamae kept her mouth shut until she had left the room again. Then she said, "Dana will get used to the idea."

"But if she's still suffering so much…"

Roselynn always had been the pushover. "I wouldn't do anything to hurt Dana," Ellamae said gruffly.

"Of course I know that. But we don't really know how she feels. And Tess is as unsure about this as we are."

We? Normally, she would have snorted at that. *She* was never unsure about anything.

But for the moment, she needed to be careful about telling certain things to softy Rose. And to Tess. She also needed to uncover a few additional facts herself. That didn't present a problem. She could always work her way around an obstacle, once she set her mind to it.

For a good cause, of course.

Tess came into the kitchen carrying a couple of tablecloths. "I'll go throw these in the laundry, Mom."

"Hold on, Tess," Ellamae said. "Got a question for you. How'd you like to be on our committee for the memorial for Paul?"

"Oh. Well…" Tess's gaze swung to her mama and back to Ellamae again. For a moment, she looked the way Rose claimed Dana had—like she didn't know where to turn. But she nodded. "Sure, I'd love to."

"Good." Ellamae smiled.

Yeah, she could always work her way around anything.

AT NOON ON TUESDAY, Dana walked the short distance from Wright Place Realty to the Double S. Her brisk pace and the warm sunshine on her shoulders made some of her tension ease. Not having seen Ben for a couple of days might have had something to do with that, too. She and Tess had worked late last night, rounding up properties for their client to view. When she arrived home, Anne said her landlord had left.

Now she turned the corner onto Signal Street and came to an abrupt stop.

Ben stood in front of the Double S, leaning against his pickup truck. Try as she might, she couldn't keep her pulse from fluttering.

After a long, deep breath, she walked up to him. "What brings you to town in the middle of a workday?"

"A long list of overdue errands. Then I figured, as long as I was here, I'd stop for a cup of coffee."

Obviously, he wasn't having issues with his ranch foreman, as Caleb was. But her heart sank. "You're just going in?"

He shook his head. "Just coming out. I've got a few things to do before I head over to your house."

"Well, so long."

She turned away. He put his hand on her wrist. His touch warmed her more completely than the sun had done—and every muscle it had relaxed now tightened again. She slid her hand free.

"What's your hurry?" he asked.

"I'm early for a meeting here, and I want to get some paperwork done."

"For your proposal?"

She should've known better than to hope he'd forgotten. That was part of the trouble with Ben. He had one of the best—and longest—memories she'd ever known. "No. I told you. We're not quite done with that yet."

"Ellamae and her buddies will be busy drawing up a proposal of their own. For Paul," he added, as if she didn't know what he'd meant. "I have to say, you didn't appear to think much about their idea the other day."

"I didn't expect to have to think about it at all," she said. "They sprang it on me out of nowhere."

"That's not much of a...reason for not showing a little more enthusiasm."

She gripped the handle of her briefcase. *"Reason?"* she repeated. "Why do I need to give you a reason for my feelings?"

He shrugged. "Okay," he conceded. "Maybe you don't.

But as you've mentioned it, how *do* you feel about it, any-how?"

She exhaled in exasperation and stared at him. "And why do you think you have the right to ask that, either?" She shook her head. "Ben, what's gotten into you?"

"I could ask you the same question. Paul is a hero, dam-mit."

Yes, she wanted to shoot back at him. *A hero to you and all the folks in town.*

Once, long ago, Paul had been her hero, too.

For as long as she had known him, he could do no wrong in anyone's eyes, including her own, from his grade school days all the way up through senior high. And after his suc-cess on the football team, he'd guaranteed his place in the town's history as their golden boy. But gold tarnished. Fame didn't last forever. Neither had her relationship with Paul.

She couldn't say that to Ben, who now stood glaring at her. She couldn't say that to anyone.

"Folks want to do something to honor him," he said, "and you don't seem to want any part of it."

His voice had risen a notch, and she cringed. She didn't intend to talk about this with him. Not now. Not ever. And especially not right here.

Footsteps sounded on the sidewalk behind her. She only hoped whoever approached hadn't heard Ben's words.

"Dana?"

The deep voice so close behind her made her jump. Turn-ing, she looked up at the new client she had met just that morning.

A very good-looking man, Jared Hall stood a smidge taller than Ben. But he didn't have Ben's broad shoulders. He didn't have Ben's sparkling dark eyes. And, she dis-covered to her dismay, he didn't thrill her the way Ben did.

"Jared Hall." He held out his hand.

Quickly, she introduced the men, who stood eyeing each other. "Well," she blurted into the silence, "I guess Jared and I should get to work."

"Yeah," Ben said, putting his hand on her wrist again. "I'll see you later."

Casual words. Words anyone might say to a friend. But his lingering touch and intimate tone gave a completely different impression. Before she could ward it off, a shiver of excitement ran through her. Disgust at herself immediately followed. He'd done that deliberately, as if to prove something to her.

Or to Jared.

Unsteadily, she turned away.

As she and Jared walked toward the Double S, she heard no movement behind her, no sound of a pickup door opening. Ben still watched them.

When Jared held open the door of the café, she looked up at him and…deliberately…gave him a wide smile. But as they entered, she didn't dare look toward the street.

Inside the café, Dori and Manny greeted her with their usual beaming smiles.

"I heard you had my pastries on Saturday," Dori said. "You enjoyed them, yes?"

"Absolutely," Dana assured her.

"Along with my tacos," Manny said. He and Dori had a friendly rivalry about which of their specialties brought customers into the Double S.

"Yes, along with the tacos," Dana said, laughing. She introduced Jared, then led him to a corner booth.

Dori followed, carrying the tea and coffee they had ordered. "Also," she said, "I hear there is big excitement in town about your Paul."

Dana tightened her grip on the paper napkin she'd just

spread across her lap. "That's right. Ellamae and some of the other folks are planning something."

"Yes, it was Ellamae who told me this morning. A very good thing. Everyone here says the same."

"Yes," she murmured.

When Dori walked away, Dana lifted her teacup and smiled across the booth at Jared, not seeing him. Her mind had gone far away in time but just a few blocks away in distance, back a year and more ago to the day she had learned of Paul's death.

The news had left her reeling. Not because of what he had meant to her but because he no longer meant anything to her at all.

Not for her sake but for their children's.

The daughter who idolized her daddy. The son who looked the image of him. And the baby she had just, days before, discovered she carried inside her.

Ben couldn't have realized what his pushing about her feelings had done to her.

Deep inside, she recognized that Paul had given his life bravely and that folks looked up to him for that sacrifice. Yet she couldn't get past her own knowledge of him.

Of the man he had never been.

Not a day passed without a bitter memory of how she'd felt about her marriage. About her husband. Still trying to deal with her disappointment in both, how could she face the idea of a statue in his honor?

BEN GOT THROUGH THE REST of his errands, then headed to where he wanted to be. Dana's house.

No, *his* house. Dana's home.

The sitter had already picked up the kids. When he drove up and parked near the garage, he found them all on the front porch. He could see Dana's van coming down the street. Couldn't have timed his arrival any better.

As he got out of the truck, P.J. ran up. "Am I helping you today, Ben?" he asked.

"You sure are."

"Good."

A second after Dana parked beside the pickup truck, the passenger door opened and Lissa and Nate spilled from the van.

Ben looked at Nate in surprise. "What are you doing here? I thought for sure you'd go right home from school to spend some time with your mama and daddy, now they're back from their trip."

"They're not home."

As the two girls ran off, Dana said, "Tess took Caleb to the airport. He's going to Montana for a couple of days."

"Did you get things taken care of with your rodeo cowboy?"

"No. In fact, we're getting together again tonight."

"Tonight? You mean, you're dating him?"

She raised her eyebrows. Well, all right, maybe he'd been a bit too blunt. But seeing the man with her hadn't set right with him. Not at all. Thinking of her going out with him...

"No, not a date. We're meeting at the office to go over some listings."

She pulled a sack from Harley's out of the back of the van.

Seeing that she'd come from the market gave him other things to think about. It reinforced the thoughts he'd had about her lately, about how much responsibility she carried now that Paul was gone. The list of jobs he'd found needed doing around this house only added to his concerns.

Since Paul's death, Dana had become a single mom, sole breadwinner and the person who needed to take care of her family. And her home. And anything else that might arise, such as the proposal she was working on. The one she still wouldn't tell him about.

She reached into the van for another grocery sack and slammed the door.

"Can I carry those for you?"

She shook her head. "It's okay, I can handle them."

Without your help, her words implied. Surprise at her attitude no longer registered with him.

P.J. had waited quietly but now burst out, "Mama, I have to help Ben today!"

"Is that so?"

"Yep." He nodded. "We can hang up the flowers you have out on the porch."

"The flowers?" she asked.

"Please, Mama." He nearly bounced up and down in his eagerness. "Then I'll have more room for my dinosaurs."

For a moment she looked distressed, and then she smiled at him and nodded. "Sure, that would be great."

"Good. But you gotta come help, too. You gotta tell us where to put the flowers."

"I do?"

Her gaze moved to Ben, as if she suspected he had put her son up to the idea. Turning, she walked toward the house, P.J. beside her. "I'll need to take care of the groceries first."

Obviously, the thought of helping them didn't appeal to her. He wasn't sure he much cared for it, either. He didn't need the torture of working that close and not being able to touch her.

By rights, he probably should stay away altogether. Yet he looked for any excuse he could find to see her again.

He ground his teeth together. He'd been seeing her all his life. Why the hell would he need an excuse to do that now?

Another concern to add to the list of those that had plagued him lately. Concern about loyalty to the best friend who had trusted him to watch over his wife and children. Concern about the compassion he felt for this woman he'd known forever and was beginning to respect more each day—this woman who had so much on her plate.

This woman who still grieved for her husband.

Clamping his jaw shut against the words he wanted to say, he followed the two of them through the house and into the kitchen.

Abruptly, P.J. backed toward the door. "I forgot. I gotta get my tools." He turned and ran from the room.

Dana began unloading the sacks. "I know he's upset about not having room to play with his toys. I intended to get around to those plants very soon." Her voice shook with anger.

"I have no doubt about that. And for the record, I had nothing to do with the idea. P.J. came up with it on his own."

She squared her shoulders and stared at him in disbelief. That did it.

"Hold off on those groceries." In a half-dozen strides, he crossed the room. "We need to talk about what's going on here."

"As in...?"

"As in, what is it with you? First, for all these months, you refused to let me do anything for you—I had to buy an office building and now this damn house to manage to help you at all. And now, you don't believe me about P.J.?"

"I didn't say that."

Once again, her voice shook. He could see the tears in her eyes. Maybe she felt as frustrated as he did. But there was something else in her face, something he had trouble reading.

That had happened more and more often lately. It bothered the hell out of him.

But right now, he didn't need to read her expression.

He put both hands on her shoulders and turned her to face him squarely. "Dana, what you said with your words and what you're saying with your body language are two different things. Why are you making this situation so hard for us?"

"Because *I* should be the one to give P.J. the space to play with his toys."

Baffled, he shook his head. "What's the difference who hangs up those plants? Not everyone wants or has the skills to do handyman chores. Or sometimes they can't do them alone. Look how many times I came over to give Paul a hand. How is my helping him back then any different from my coming here to help you now?"

"I don't—"

Need your help.

He could hear the words. Before she could say them, he reached up to touch his fingertip above her upper lip. It silenced her immediately—a good thing, because as the warmth of her skin jolted through him, he had to pull his hand away.

Later, he'd worry about the reaction. Now he couldn't let it distract him. He let the safer feeling of irritation take over again.

He leaned forward, looking into her wide blue eyes. "You can't turn away from more than twenty years of friendship. Or at least, I can't. If you won't take help from me for yourself, at least accept it for your kids."

"I have been, haven't I?" As if she suddenly fought a smile, one corner of her mouth twitched. "Lord knows, Clarice and Ellamae think you've become a permanent boarder here."

P.J. ran into the kitchen. "Ready!" He shook the plastic canister Ben had given him, making the washers rattle. "C'mon, let's go." He grabbed Ben's hand and tugged. "C'mon, Mama."

"As soon as I finish unpacking the groceries," she told him. "You two go ahead."

"Okay."

P.J. pulled harder, and Ben let himself be towed through the kitchen and out the door. Once on the porch, the boy kept busy running back and forth to the picnic table, moving his dinosaurs out of harm's way.

Ben welcomed the breathing space, the chance to get his thoughts together. If he could.

Before, he'd had a long list of questions. Those, he'd understood. What he couldn't deal with now was the thought that had raced through his mind when he'd touched Dana. And the added wagonload of guilt that had followed.

He didn't want to be her boy next door any longer. He wanted a chance with her—and he aimed to get it.

Chapter Nine

Between the two of them, Dana and Tess had kept Jared on the run to various properties all around the state. On Friday, they met at the office to plan their weekend strategy.

"He's mine for the rest of the afternoon," Dana said. "The owner of that property outside Tucumcari called, and we're going down there to meet with him."

If not for being away from the kids, she wouldn't have minded the long ride. On the other hand, it gave her something she wanted. An excuse to stay busy. In these few days since she had helped Ben and P.J. with the flowers out on the porch, she'd needed something to occupy her mind. To keep her from dwelling on that afternoon. Ben's reminder of all the times he'd come by the house to help Paul had stirred up too many memories for her to think about.

His touch had stirred up too many emotions for her to handle.

"You're awfully preoccupied," Tess said.

She'd spoken in a teasing tone. Still, the words startled Dana. She hoped the reaction hadn't shown in her face. That wouldn't do. She needed to be very careful with Tess. With Ben. With everyone.

"You also seem awfully eager to escort Jared around in the afternoons." Tess smiled. "And I heard you went out with him last night. Are you sure you're not angling for more than dinner invitations with him? He's a good-looking man."

Dana forced a laugh. "The only thing I'm angling for is to give you and Caleb more newlywed time now that he's back from Montana. After all, you're still pretty much on your honeymoon, aren't you?"

Now, it was Tess's turn to laugh. "Yes, that's true. So I guess I'll head back home. You'll be picking Jared up at the Whistlestop?"

She nodded. "I'll be right behind you."

"Okay. But you know…" Tess's tone turned serious. "It's not a bad thing if you're interested in a man again."

"Tess, please don't."

"Okay, I won't. For now. Then, on another subject, do you and Kayla plan to present your proposal Monday night?"

"Yes."

"Good. I can't wait till you get it approved. I don't know why no one else ever thought of building a playground in town. But it's a great idea."

"We think so, too," she said, pouncing on the new topic. "I expect you and Caleb will be able to make use of it one of these days soon. And I don't mean for Nate, either."

Tess grinned. "I sure hope so. But it might be a little while before we need to think about that. Anyhow, I'm sure the council will go for the idea, hands down. Speaking of which…" she paused, then went on "…I'm on the committee for the other proposal. For the memorial in Paul's memory—"

Dana tried not to cringe.

"—and they asked me to find out if you'd like to join us."

"Oh." Avoiding her friend's eye, she reached for the pen she'd left lying on her desk. "Please," she began, "tell them I appreciate that they asked, but…but I think it would be best for the group to make their decisions without me. Besides, Kayla and I already have our proposal."

Tess nodded. "I thought you might turn us down," she said softly, "but folks wanted you to know they'd offered."

After Tess left the office, Dana slumped back in her chair and groaned.

What had she set herself up for? What kind of a tangled mess had she made with her web of deceit?

With all her efforts to hide the truth about Paul, she had never expected things to come to this. To the bizarre twist brought about by her misplaced pride. And by everyone's misperceptions of her marriage.

She didn't want to be held up as the iconic war widow. She didn't want any part of their tribute at all.

How could she have said any of that to Tess?

She couldn't, and there was no use even thinking about it.

She pushed herself upright and grabbed the phone on her desk. Then she punched the speed dial for her home number and sat biting her lip while the line engaged.

Ben had said he would be by around this time. He might already have arrived. Fortunately, she was going far away in another direction, and he'd be long gone by the time she got home.

The babysitter answered the phone on the second ring.

"Yep, everything is fine here," Anne said. "And since you're going to be a little late tonight, I've challenged P.J. to a checkers marathon. That'll keep him from bothering Lissa."

"That's great, Anne, thanks. I'll have my cell on if you need me." Dana hung up the office phone and pulled her handbag out from the bottom drawer of her desk.

Time to head over to the Whistlestop Inn to pick up the man who had so recently entered her life.

Time to stop thinking about the man who had always been part of it.

LONG HOURS LATER, Dana dropped off their client at the Whistlestop.

"Thanks for everything, Jared."

Their trip out of town had taken much longer than she'd anticipated. He and the ranch owner had hit it off, and their meeting had led to an invitation for a late, lengthy supper.

On the return trip, still hours from Flagman's Folly, the battery of her van had died. In the harsh, dry heat of the Southwest, batteries didn't last that long to begin with. Neither did a few dozen other parts of a vehicle. The wear and tear of a job that took her all over the state only added to the chances of something going wrong.

"I'm glad you weren't alone," he said.

"Me, too. This could've happened at any time. I was lucky."

"We both were." He smiled at her. "I enjoyed the trip."

She smiled back and watched him go up the steps of the inn. When the door closed behind him, she turned the van in the direction of home. They had been lucky, also, to find a mechanic willing to come and tow the van back to his garage, where she bought the new battery.

Between all that and the long ride home, it was now well after 2 a.m. She wanted nothing more than to get back to the house, kiss her kids and crawl into bed.

Again, she felt guilty about being away from the kids for so long, although since Paul's death, they'd gotten used to being left with a sitter in the evenings once in a while. Anne had put them to bed on more than one occasion.

She'd called home several times to check in and was relieved to hear that everything had been going well.

But after all Anne's reassurances, she now felt surprised—and concerned—when she pulled up in front of the house and saw Ben's truck still beside the garage.

Leaving her van in the driveway, she hurried across the lawn. If not for the time, the sight of the truck wouldn't have alarmed her. Ben always wanted to wrap up a project the same day, if he could. But he'd never stayed this late before.

She nearly tripped going up the steps. It took her a couple of tries to fit her key into the lock. When she finally pushed the door open, the sight in the living room froze her in place.

Ben lay sprawled on the couch, watching television. Seeing him so relaxed lowered her anxiety immediately. But why hadn't he left? Frowning, she asked, "Are the kids okay?"

"Fine. All upstairs in their beds, asleep."

"Good. But where's Anne? And what are you doing here?"

"She didn't want to let you down, but when you called and said you'd be home so late, she finally told me she had a hot date waiting. I volunteered to stay." He yawned widely. "To answer your question, I'm the replacement babysitter."

She bit her lip. Much as she wished she hadn't come home to find him here, she couldn't argue about his stepping in this time. Though she trusted Anne, this late at night, she appreciated having a responsible adult in the house.

Adults couldn't come much more responsible than Ben.

And men couldn't come much sexier.

His hair tumbled on his forehead as if he'd run his fingers through it a dozen times. His eyes looked heavy-lidded from fighting off sleep.

Slowly, quietly, she closed the door behind her and advanced into the room. "Thank you," she said.

"You're welcome." After tossing the television remote onto the coffee table, he scrubbed his face with his hands. "The van held out all the way back here?"

"Yes, as I told Anne on the phone, it was just the battery."

"Guess I'd better head home," he said. He yawned again.

"You don't look like you're in any shape to drive."

"I'll be fine."

She glanced toward the stairway, took a deep breath and looked back at him again. "Why don't you stay the night," she suggested. "That is, for what's left of it."

He stared at her for a long moment, his eyes half-closed, an unreadable expression on his face. Or maybe it was just fatigue.

"I'll be fine," he said again.

"I'd rather not have you take the chance." A sudden case of nerves made her babble. "You look dead on your feet— or you would if you could stand up, and I'm not completely sure you can do that. There aren't any empty beds in the house, but you can spend the rest of the night here on the couch."

Her final word hung in the air. Neither of them needed the reminder. But that was over. Done with. It wouldn't happen again. She *would not* think about it.

And it was crazy to feel this anxious about inviting him to stay. Late as it was, she'd planned to insist that Anne sleep over until the morning, anyhow. Did it really matter that Paul's best friend and not her babysitter slept in her living room?

"Honestly, Ben. I appreciate your helping out tonight, and I wouldn't want to feel responsible for something happening to you on the way home just because you stuck around to watch over my kids. You can have the couch— it's no big deal. You've slept on it before." She took another breath, let it out and added, "After all, we're friends, aren't we?"

And after all, it wasn't as though she was proposition-ing him.

His sudden piercing look made her wonder if he'd thought exactly that.

She dropped her bag onto the nearest chair. "You're stay-ing," she said firmly.

After yawning once more, he shrugged and reached for the hem of his T-shirt. In one swift movement he pulled the shirt over his head, exposing lots of lean, tanned skin.

She moved toward the stairs. "I'll just run up and get you some linens."

Run described her escape from the room perfectly.

Even while staring at Ben on that couch, she'd managed to keep all the memories of their night together out of her mind. But once he'd pulled off his T-shirt... Once she'd seen him half-naked in the dark intimacy of the living room lit only by the glow of a small lamp and the television screen... The sight had done something wild to her pulse. And the memories had flooded her mind.

It's only good old Ben, she told herself, hands shaking as she sorted through her linen closet. But the reminder didn't work this time.

To her dismay, she had a feeling it would never work again.

ALONE IN HER BED a little while later, Dana struggled to calm her breathing. And her racing thoughts. Awareness of her unexpected guest downstairs troubled her. But she had to confess Ben's nearness excited her, too.

At long last, she fell into a restless, dream-filled sleep.

She was abruptly awakened from it, first by the sound of P.J.'s bedroom slippers slapping on the stairs and then by his exuberant greeting. He'd just discovered Ben in the living room.

If the brightness of her room didn't tell her she'd over-slept, one look at her alarm clock did.

She exhaled in exasperation. Seven-thirty. But after all, it was Saturday. By rights, she couldn't actually resent that Ben had slept in, considering he'd been up so late only to help her out. On the other hand, he should have been long gone before any of the kids were up.

Especially Lissa. Since their talk, Dana had kept a close eye on her daughter, who still seemed irritated by having Ben around. Finding him there when she first woke up wouldn't improve her disposition any! With luck, Lissa would sleep in as usual on a Saturday, and Ben *would* be gone by the time she came downstairs.

She slid her arms into her robe and tied it tightly around her. Quickly, she went to the head of the stairs and looked down into the living room.

She could just see Ben on the couch with the sheets rum-pled around him, the pale yellow fabric highlighting his dark hair and tanned skin. His hair was even more tousled this morning, making him look younger and bringing back a flood of memories.

Ben with his hair dripping water onto his face the day at Sidewinder Creek when they'd all learned to swim.

With his clothes tousled after the entire seventh grade had camped out on his daddy's ranch.

With his eyes shining when he'd come to visit at the hos-pital the night Lissa was born.

Those and other memories—too many memories—she didn't want to think about.

Instead, she went down the stairs and focused on P.J., who sat leaning against the arm of the couch, his feet braced on Ben's thigh. He gestured with both hands and spoke at top speed. "And we were on this *huge* checkerboard, Ben! There were dinosaurs all over, too. They *flew* down the mountain—and then they landed. And they *smooshed* all the flowers flat like pancakes!"

"Really?" Ben asked. His lips tightened. She knew he was holding back a laugh. "That's one heck of a dream, buddy."

"Yep. It was fun." Spotting Dana, he grinned. "Mama, Ben played checkers with me all night."

"Not quite. Only till bedtime," Ben clarified, exchanging glances with her.

"I guess I owe you another thank-you."

"Why? It's not like it's the first time I've played games with the kids."

She stopped those memories before they could start.

"If you feel the need for more thanks," he continued, "I'll take them for dealing with Stacey's diaper last night."

When he grinned, she bit her lip to keep from smiling back.

P.J. squealed. "You changed Stacey's *dirty diaper?*"

Ben nodded. "Sure did. I changed yours once or twice when you were her age, too."

"Ew-w-w-w."

The doorbell rang. Undoubtedly happy for the distraction, P.J. slid from the edge of the couch and ran toward the entryway.

The sound of the bell had made Dana anything but happy. Who on earth would come calling at this hour?

Ben raised one eyebrow, probably thinking the same thing. He sat back and rested one bare arm along the back of the couch as if settling in for a nice, long conversation with whoever had rung the bell.

She swallowed a moan. He could—and did—talk to anyone, anytime. But obviously he hadn't thought twice about who might find him sitting on her living room couch. Could she somehow casually ask him to leave the room? Or at least to put his T-shirt back on?

And call attention to the fact that she'd noticed—and been bothered by—his half-nakedness?

No, she couldn't.

She tugged on her belt again. P.J. looked through the side window and then rushed to throw the door wide open. He knew better than to do that with a stranger, which meant the visitor had to be someone he knew.

Did that make this situation better or worse? It wouldn't matter either way, if she could just keep the person outside. She hurried to join P.J.

Her next-door neighbor stood on the doorstep. Dana's annoyance evaporated immediately. "Clarice, are you okay?"

"I was about to ask you the same question. Just thought I'd check…" She looked Dana over from head to toe. Then she peered around P.J. into the living room. *"Ben?"* She proceeded to look *him* over from head to…torso.

In spite of the situation, Dana found herself holding back a laugh. Clarice's inspection had definitely come to a halt at chest level. Eighty-five years old, and the woman obviously still recognized a good thing when she saw it.

P.J. lost interest and wandered toward the kitchen.

Clarice's gaze met hers again.

For a moment she held on to hope that only idle nosiness had brought the older woman here this morning. Hopes that Clarice's suddenly steely gaze squashed flat as P.J.'s floral pancake.

"My goodness. And in front of the *children?*"

She gasped. "It's not what you're thinking."

"No, it's what I'm seeing. Ben's truck in the driveway. *All* night."

"I had some car trouble yesterday. He stayed with the

kids for me." Her heart sank. Within the hour, Ellamae would hear about her overnight visitor. Then the word would spread all over town.

"You want to be careful." Clarice sent a meaningful glance toward Ben. "Both of you."

"Dana's right, Clarice," he said easily. "The situation isn't what you're thinking. And it would be a real shame to have rumors start just because I gave Dana a helping hand out of pure friendship. Wouldn't it?"

"Friendship?" She looked him over again and shook her head. "I need to get back home."

As she stalked away, Dana closed the door gently, knowing she hadn't heard the end of this. And she had only herself to blame for insisting that Ben stay.

P.J. trotted in from the kitchen. "C'mon, Ben. Mama will make breakfast soon."

"We'll be there in a minute, sweetie," she said. "Get the place mats on the table for me, please."

"Okay."

When he had left, she walked slowly into the living room, looked at Ben and raised her brows. "I've watched you talk a nervous mare across Sidewinder Creek in the middle of a gullywasher," she said, "but I think you've lost your touch."

He rose from the couch. Suddenly she felt the overwhelming urge to hurry into the kitchen with P.J. Somehow she managed to stand her ground.

"What makes you say that?"

She choked on a laugh. "Do you really think Clarice will keep quiet about finding you here this morning?"

He shrugged and spread his arms wide. His biceps bulged and his triceps did something equally devastating, and suddenly she lost all desire to laugh.

"C'mon, Dana. What do I look like? A fortune-teller?"

"No. Like a man who had better put his T-shirt back on if he plans to eat breakfast at *my* table."

There. She'd said it.

And now, though she didn't quite flee, she racewalked into the kitchen, mentally kicking herself the entire way. She hadn't planned to invite him to stay for breakfast, but the words had come out of her mouth faster than she could think.

His half-naked state had driven her to it.

Grabbing a jar of baby food from the refrigerator, she pressed it against her heat-flushed cheek. The chilled glass helped cool her down a bit. But nothing could stop the rush of guilt and shame that filled her.

She and Ben hadn't lied. The situation *wasn't* what Clarice had thought—at least, not this morning. Still, her neighbor's suspicions hit too close for comfort. For safety.

Whether or nor Clarice had proof of an indiscretion didn't matter. She would never keep gossip like this to herself.

"ARE WE WORKING TODAY, Ben?" P.J. asked halfway through breakfast.

"We sure are." He ate a mouthful of French toast and considered the situation he found himself in.

Last night, after Dana and the client were safely on their way back to Flagman's Folly, he'd given a big sigh of relief. And he'd felt inordinately pleased at how the rest of his evening turned out.

It hadn't taken much effort to convince her sitter he didn't mind her going. Truth be told, if she hadn't left, he'd have stayed anyway. He didn't care to leave a teenager alone at that hour with the kids.

On the other hand, when Dana had finally arrived, he'd found he didn't much like the idea of being alone with her,

either. In her dark, quiet living room, he'd gotten to thinking—probably about the same things Clarice had thought.
Even though he owned this house, Dana would have kicked
him out of the place if he'd tried to put those thoughts into
action.

Still, he'd been happy to bed down on the couch for the
rest of the night. It fit right in with his plans for the weekend.

Besides, she made a great breakfast.

"Do you want more bacon?" P.J. asked, pushing the platter toward Ben's end of the kitchen table.

"Sure. Thanks, buddy." He took another couple of slices
and passed the platter to Lissa, sitting opposite her brother.

When she'd first seen him in the kitchen, she'd acted
a little standoffish but now seemed to have warmed up to
him again.

Dana, on the other hand, had gotten colder. She'd taken
a seat at the far end of the table, next to Stacey's high chair.
She hadn't said much once they'd all come into the kitchen.
Come to think of it, she hadn't even made eye contact with
him since they'd sat down.

His feeling of pleasure gave way to guilt.

Leftover guilt from last night, at the way he'd played
up his sleepiness. Sure, he'd had a long day and could easily have nodded out on the couch, but he wasn't as tired as
he'd let on.

Then more guilt this morning, at lounging around instead of getting up and heading out the door. Leaving when
he should have wouldn't have changed anything as far as
Dana's next-door neighbor was concerned, but at least Clarice wouldn't have woken up to see his truck still in the
driveway.

That was six of one, half a dozen of another, though. He

would've gone home, showered and eaten breakfast in his own kitchen. But eventually, he'd have come back.

He still had errands to run and chores to do at the ranch this weekend, but he intended to spend what time he could right here. The more Dana saw of him, the more she'd get used to having him around. And the easier it would make it for him to get closer to her.

Already his plan had begun to work—she'd invited him to stay for breakfast, hadn't she?

P.J. held the nearly empty bottle of syrup out to him. "We need more, please."

He smiled. The kids didn't need time to get used to him.

"I'll take care of it," Dana said.

He had already risen. "No problem. I've got it."

"Ben knows where to find everything," Lissa said matter-of-factly.

"That's true." On his way over to the pantry closet, he thought about all the time he'd once spent in this house. Even in the few months just after Paul's death, he'd been a constant visitor…until Dana had started coming up with reasons to turn him away.

"Mama, you went out with Mr. Hall yesterday, didn't you?" she asked.

"Yes, I took him to look at property."

"Like you did with Caleb?"

"That's right."

"He's a rodeo star, too, just like Caleb."

"Yes, he is," her mama agreed.

Lissa's eyes shone with the same rodeo fever Nate and the rest of their friends had caught. Having Caleb Cantrell return to town was probably the most exciting thing they'd ever had happen in their young lives.

In her mind, a plain, everyday rancher just couldn't compare to the excitement of a real, live rodeo star.

She put her hands flat on the table and leaned toward her mama. "You really think Mr. Hall will buy a ranch here, just the way Caleb did?"

"I certainly hope so."

He frowned down at his plate. Now that Dana couldn't rightly keep him out of his own house, he suspected she'd begun to use her job as a way to avoid him when he came here to work in the evenings. But she'd just sounded as eager as Lissa had about the idea of a new star in town. Her tone reminded him how much she could use another big sale.

Why the hell that meant she had to have supper with the man, he didn't know.

"Mama," P.J. said, "Ben looks sad. I think you better make him more French toast."

He looked up to find Dana staring at him. Quickly, he glanced toward her son. "I'm not sad at all, just thinking of how many chores I'm going to have to do today to work off this good breakfast."

He'd thought of a few other things, as well. And he didn't much like the direction his mind had headed.

Maybe Dana didn't worry about the size of her commission when she drove her new client all over the state. Maybe she hadn't minded getting stranded with the man last night, either. Maybe her interest in him was just what she'd said to Lissa: she hoped he would settle down in the area.

Trying not to frown again, he pushed his empty plate away from him.

For the first time, he wondered if Dana had a touch of rodeo fever, too.

Chapter Ten

Dana stared through the kitchen window into the backyard.

Right after breakfast, Ben had taken P.J. to the far end of the property, where he had begun breaking ground to lay in a row of fence posts. He'd settled P.J. off to one side of his work area with a small plastic bucket and shovel.

After a couple of quick peeks through the kitchen curtains, she began to feel as bad as Clarice and Ellamae with their spying. But that didn't stop her from looking....

P.J. ran back and forth, filling his bucket and then emptying it at the base of a small tree.

The digging was dirty work. Hot work, too, even though it was still early morning. As she peered through the window again, she saw Ben had stripped off his T-shirt and stood wiping his forehead with the back of his hand.

Her own hand stilled on the insulated cooler she had just filled with lemonade. She bit her lip in indecision. Half of her knew she should bring the cold drink to him. The other half warned she'd best not go outside.

Ignoring the warning, she picked up the cooler and a couple of plastic mugs and crossed to the kitchen door.

When he saw her coming, he set his shovel aside.

"Looks like you've been working hard," she said. "You've made a lot of progress."

"Yeah. Slow progress, but I'm not taking any chances on doing anything I shouldn't."

Good advice. She'd do well to take it herself. The skin on her neck prickled, as if Clarice stared at her from next door. But what could she find wrong in Dana offering her landlord cold lemonade?

Ben gave her a half smile that left her insides shivering. That answered her question, all right.

He took the mug and tipped his head back to drink from it. She watched the muscles of his throat work as he polished off the contents in one long, uninterrupted swallow.

Almost unaware of doing it, she swallowed, too.

When he'd finished, he swept his tongue along the splash of lemonade left on his upper lip.

Her mouth suddenly felt as dry and cakey as the dirt around them. She swallowed again and wished she'd brought a mug outside for herself.

P.J. tugged on her arm. "What about me, Mama? I worked hard, too."

Face flushing, she turned to him. How could she have let herself get so distracted, she'd neglected her own child? "Right here," she said, handing him the smaller mug.

Then she refilled Ben's and again found herself frozen, watching as he took another drink.

She told herself to stop staring—and her self argued back. *Why should I stop? I'll make sure nothing ever happens between us again.* Still, the thoughts she kept having about Ben, the reactions she kept fighting were all perfectly natural, perfectly normal—even if she *could* think back almost far enough to recall them both in diapers.

But those days were long gone. Now, she was a full grown adult female.

And he was one hot-looking male.

She ran her tongue across her lips. A sponge-dry tongue

that left her longing to take a swig directly from the insulated cooler.

She could just imagine the uproar she'd get from P.J., who had heard her lecture on that more than once.

Wasn't this just wonderful! Not only had Ben shaken her normal reserve, he had managed to undermine her parenting skills—without even knowing he was doing so.

"You okay?" he asked.

She started, realizing that he had noticed her staring at him. She said the first thing that came to her mind. "You've got dirt on your face."

Looking down, he clapped his free hand against his jeans, raising a cloud of dust, and laughed. "I can't see myself worrying about a smudge or two when I'm covered head to toe in the stuff."

"I suppose you're right."

"P.J. said I'll need to take a shower when I'm done. Didn't you, buddy?" He directed the question to her son but kept his gaze fixed on her.

She had a sudden vision of a steamy shower door and Ben's naked body half-visible through it.

"Yep," P.J. confirmed. "Mama says when we come in dirty, we should go right in and wash up."

Ben raised one eyebrow, as if challenging her to deny her son's words.

She bit her tongue. Again, somehow, he had turned her parenting skills to work in his favor. This time, she felt certain he knew exactly what he'd done.

"I've got a couple of things to take care of around noon," he told her. "I'll plan to stop and shower up before then. I've got a change of clothes out in the truck," he added. "You won't even have to provide a towel. I've got one of those, too."

The image *that* brought to mind was not something she wanted to think about then. "Don't be silly," she snapped. "I can certainly give you a towel."

He grinned.

Clamping her jaw tight, she glared at him. No doubt about his challenge now. Whether or not she'd planned to offer him the use of the shower no longer mattered. Because now she couldn't refuse. She'd gone right along with *his* plan, just as he had intended.

He reached for the T-shirt he had tossed onto a mound of dirt and used it to wipe the sweat from his face.

Immediately, P.J. grabbed the hem of his own shirt and scrubbed his chin with it.

She tightened her grip on the cooler. "All done with that?" she asked, gesturing toward Ben's mug. He nodded and handed it to her. "I guess I'll get back to the house."

"I guess I'll be getting back to work. At least, until it's time for that shower."

Gritting her teeth, she walked away.

Trust Ben to find something to tease her with and run with it. He'd been doing that since he was four years old. She should have been used to it by now. She shouldn't have reacted.

He couldn't have meant to add sexual undertones to their perfectly innocent conversation. Not after their run-in with Clarice earlier!

His teasing aside, though, Ben was a good man. She couldn't deny that. Again, she saw her son copying Ben's move with the T-shirt. He made a good role model for any little boy, and especially one like P.J., who no longer had a daddy.

It was the other images of Ben imprinted on her brain that

had left her shaken. His wide, easy grin. His dirt-smeared but handsome face. His sweaty, hard-muscled body.

The body that would soon stand naked in her downstairs shower.

A WHILE LATER, DANA FOUND herself pacing the kitchen floor. She desperately needed something to help burn up her nervous energy.

Like baking.

Yes. Measuring and mixing ingredients would distract her. Inhaling the sweet smells of sugar and vanilla would settle her nerves. Would keep her from dwelling on thoughts she didn't want to think about. From obsessing over emotions she didn't want to feel.

Quickly she washed her hands and assembled what she needed for the kids' most often requested cookie, a recipe she'd created herself. She'd always loved to bake, and it seemed as though she never had much time for it lately. Going through the familiar motions relaxed her.

Until she heard the footsteps on the back porch steps. Solid footsteps. Not P.J. in his sneakers, but the heavier tread of an adult. She fumbled the measuring cup in her fingers, spilling flour across the breakfast bar. So much for settling her nerves.

Bracing herself, she turned.

It wasn't Ben on the porch.

Her next-door neighbor peered through the screen door.

And a different kind of tension filled Dana.

"Come on in, Clarice," she called. Swiping at the counter with a damp cloth, she cleaned up the spilled flour.

The other woman took a seat at the breakfast bar and placed a large leather-covered folder in front of her. "I've brought something to show you." She sounded grim.

"Give me a minute." Dana washed her hands, then came to stand beside her.

The folder turned out to be a double photo frame holding two glossy, black-and-white photographs. The left-hand photo showed a solemn-faced man with close-cropped hair wearing an army dress uniform, the jacket decorated with rows of medals.

"My Vernon," Clarice said.

Dana smiled and nodded. "I know. He didn't change much over the years, did he? Except for letting his hair grow out."

"He never could stand having that military cut."

The second frame showed him with his arm around a younger, glowing Clarice. Instead of an elaborate white gown, she wore a simple light-colored suit with a small corsage.

"I've seen these on the table in your living room," Dana said. "That's the Vernon I knew. He always had a smile."

"Yes, he did. And we had a wonderful wedding, though no one had many reasons for smiling in those days."

Those days, Dana knew, meant during World War II.

"We didn't have time to plan a formal reception." Clarice shook her head. "We didn't even have a real honeymoon. Not then. Vernon headed off to war three days later."

Dana put her hand on Clarice's shoulder and gave a gentle, comforting squeeze.

"And you're right about seeing these pictures," the older woman said. "I keep them in my parlor to remind me of Vernon." She looked sideways and added, "I've noticed you don't have a single picture of Paul around the house."

At the accusation in her tone, Dana stiffened. As casually as she could, she rounded the breakfast bar and reached for her wooden spoon. "It's…still difficult for me to look at pictures of Paul." On the surface, every word held nothing but truth. It was only the real meaning behind her state-ment that filled her with guilt. "The kids have photos of him in their bedrooms."

"That's good to hear. You can't let them forget what a good man their daddy was. Such a brave soldier, and such a big hero."

Not in Dana's eyes. But how could she tell that to Cla-rice, whose own war hero lived up to that praise?

"I know how you feel, Dana—"

She couldn't know. Not, as P.J. would say, in a million-bazillion years.

"—but you should have his picture out where you can all see it, as a family." Clarice's expression matched her stern tone.

More footsteps sounded on the back steps, this time clearly the slap of her son's sneakers accompanied by the thump of Ben's workboots. Several thuds followed, two heavy, two lighter.

"It sounds like they're leaving their dirty shoes outside," Clarice said. "At least you've got them *both* trained right."

Dana gritted her teeth at this easy assumption that Ben spent enough time here to be trained along with her son.

The screen door burst open and P.J. slid across the floor in his stocking feet. "Look at me—I'm ice-skating!"

"So you are," Clarice said.

Ben came into the room carrying P.J.'s lemonade mug. He closed the door softly behind him. His hair lay in damp waves. His chest held a sheen of perspiration.

Dana forced her gaze away. Catching P.J.'s eye, she glanced meaningfully at his socks and tried for a light tone. "It's a good thing I just mopped the floor this morn-ing, isn't it?"

"Uh-huh. Makes better ice." He climbed onto the stool

beside Clarice's. "Yippee! Ben, Mama's making her best-est cookies."

Ben moved up to stand beside her. He smelled faintly of a mixture of earth and clean, male sweat. Gripping her spoon more tightly, she berated herself for the silly thought. Was there even such a thing as "male sweat," anyway?

"I like cookies," Ben said. "What kind are these?" he asked P.J.

"Spice cookies. You'll like 'em, Ben. *Hey.*" P.J. leaned against Clarice's arm to look at the photo frame she had set to one side of the counter. "Is that my daddy?"

"No," she said, "it's—"

"I can show you my daddy." He slid from his stool and rushed toward the door.

"No running in the house," Dana called after him.

"Yes, indeed," Clarice said. "One wrong slip, and who knows what would happen." She looked levelly from her to Ben and back.

"What's that?" he asked, pointing at the frame.

Dana stared down, mixing her cookie dough. Keeping her thoughts focused on her son.

She didn't worry about P.J. carrying the photo from upstairs. He would bring the small, unframed picture he kept on the nightstand near his bed. The larger glass-and-wood-framed photo hung on the wall well out of his reach, and he knew better than to try to get to that.

Still, she didn't want him to carry down even that small photo of Paul. She didn't want Clarice to go on listing Paul's virtues. And she especially didn't want his best friend hovering near her elbow.

Just thinking of all she couldn't control made her hands shake. Trying to hide the fact, she worked doggedly with her dough, shaping the mounds into logs.

P.J. came back into the room. Lissa followed close behind.

"Here's my daddy!" He thrust the photo at Clarice.

As she took it from him, her eyes softened. Dana didn't need to guess why. The photo of Paul was almost a duplicate of the one taken of Clarice's husband, the standard, shoulders-squared pose of a soldier in full dress uniform. Like Vernon, Paul wore a row of medals on his jacket.

No matter what else he hadn't done, no matter that he'd never been the daddy her kids deserved, he'd left her children something they could view with pride.

"He's my daddy, too," Lissa said, her eyes shining. "And he's a hero. Isn't he, Mama?"

Startled, Dana mangled the log of cookie dough in her fingers. Again Ben stood watching her. This time he didn't turn away. He was waiting for her to answer. Wanting to know what she would say. She took a deep breath, hoping—praying—to come up with something that would satisfy him.

Before she could think of anything, Clarice wrapped an arm around Lissa and said, "Of course he's a hero, sweetheart. Just like my Vernon. Your daddy's someone you can be proud of. Someone we *all* need to respect."

Lissa nodded. "Just like Caleb. And Mr. Hall," she said. "They're rodeo heroes, aren't they, Mama?"

"Yes," she said, relieved to find something she could agree with. Happy to have had someone step in once again and help her by responding when she had no clue what to say. "Yes," she repeated. "They definitely are heroes."

And she definitely couldn't keep relying on other people to save her. She needed to stand up for herself. Besides, one of these days, her luck would run out—if it hadn't already.

Ben continued to stand and watch her as though he could read every thought that raced through her mind.

Tearing her gaze away, she went to the refrigerator. Once the dough had chilled, she would slice it into nice, even rounds. If only her life could turn out as perfectly. But hadn't she made sure it wouldn't? In fact, hadn't she gone out of her way to guarantee just the opposite would happen?

Her neighbor's certainty of Paul's virtues was no one's fault but her own. She ought to feel glad about it. After all, it proved that she had successfully done what she'd attempted to do—uphold the story of her ideal marriage.

A story based more on fiction than on fact.

"I need to run out to my truck," Ben said. "P.J., you'd best go and wash up."

The kids disappeared in one direction and he went off in the other. The screen door slapped closed behind him, leaving Dana with Stacey and Clarice.

The older woman didn't waste any time. "Dana," she snapped, "how can you compare a cowboy who rides bulls for a living to a man who has given service to his country the way my Vernon did? And to a man who has given his life, as Paul has?"

"I didn't mean—"

"I just hope the town council sees fit to approve our memorial." She shook her head. "Your children need something to help them remember their daddy. They won't find it here."

"Clarice!" She tried to soften her tone. "I know you have their best interests at heart. So do I, and—"

"*Really?* I can't imagine how what *I* saw this morning proves you care for your children." Her eyes glittering, she snatched up the photo frame. "You should be ashamed. Their daddy's a hero and a veteran. And though he's barely settled in his grave, you're throwing yourself at his best friend."

Clarice stormed out the back door.

Struggling to catch her breath, Dana took Stacey from the high chair and hurried from the kitchen. She couldn't stay there and face Ben when he came back inside. She couldn't stay there when the older woman's words still echoed in the room.

Beneath all the fury, Dana had heard the frustration. She'd seen the gleam of tears. Clarice *did* have her family's best interests at heart.

Knowing that, how could she just ignore what her neighbor had said? She couldn't.

Not when all the folks in town believed it, too.

Not when she was guilty of each and every accusation.

FINISHED TUCKING IN his T-shirt, Ben caught sight of himself in the mirror and nearly winced. Before his shower, he'd gone out to his truck for his duffel bag. Clarice had cornered him there, her expression looking about as grim as his reflection did now.

When she'd arrived at Dana's doorstep that morning, he hadn't known whether to laugh or groan. He should've realized she'd see the truck outside. To tell the truth, maybe he'd wanted her to notice it. Like Dana, folks needed to get used to seeing him around here.

He hadn't anticipated the older woman's reaction then. And he hadn't been ready for her anger when she'd caught him outside. She'd torn a strip off his hide over finding him on Dana's couch. Over what all the folks in town would think about "Ben Sawyer cavorting with his best friend's wife."

He'd managed to calm her down again. He thought.

If only he could settle down himself. Could shake off the guilt that stuck to him like the damp hair clinging to his forehead.

As he finished loading up his duffel bag, P.J. came to the bathroom door, providing a much-needed distraction.

"Cookies are almost ready," he said.

"Sounds good." He straightened the bath towel on the rack and grabbed the bag. "Do you think I'll be able to eat more than you will?" he asked as they walked down the hall.

"No way! I can eat a million-bazillion."

The doorbell rang, and P.J. changed direction.

He and Lissa ran in a dead heat to the front door. Squabbling over who would get to open it, they both grabbed hold of the handle and yanked. Tess stood on the doorstep with Nate.

P.J. rolled his eyes and headed toward the kitchen.

The two girls plopped down on the couch. Dana had long ago taken away the sheets Ben had left in a pile at one end.

She had just come into the room. As P.J. passed her, she smiled and ruffled his hair, then looked at Tess. "Good morning. What are you two doing here?"

"My new husband hijacked our client for the day. Nate and I are on our way to the Double S for lunch."

P.J. stopped in his tracks. "Yay! Can we go, too?"

"P.J.!" Dana said in dismay. "Wait until you're invited."

Tess laughed. "That's exactly why we stopped here. You're all invited. Our treat. P.J., how did you know?"

"I'm a good guesser." He plopped into the rocking chair.

Ben turned to Tess. "I hear you're on the proposal committee for Paul's memorial." From the corner of his eye, he saw Dana stiffen. She refused to open up about her own proposal. The fact still rankled. That was only half of it, though.

After the discussion at the Whistlestop, he'd decided to let her think over the suggestion Ellamae had made. Almost a full week ago, and it seemed she hadn't gotten comfortable with the idea yet. How the hell much time did she need to accept something she should have approved in a heartbeat?

"Where did you hear the news?" Tess asked.

"From Clarice." He shot Dana another look. Her frozen

expression said the woman had cornered her alone, too. "She was visiting here and mentioned it."

Tess nodded. "Instead of a statue, we're now thinking of a monument of some kind. Whatever we decide," she said, smiling, "Caleb said he would provide the funds for it."

"Hey," he protested, "I'm willing to foot the bill."

"Oh, I knew you would be. But Caleb volunteered. He wants to repay folks for their kindness since he's come home."

Abruptly Dana turned and went toward the kitchen.

Startled, he stared after her. For the first time, his conviction wavered. Maybe he'd misjudged her lack of enthusiasm over the memorial. Maybe she'd had the same thoughts that had just slammed into his mind at Tess's words.

Caleb had returned to town.

But Paul would never come home again.

Dana reappeared carrying Stacey. "I've got the first batch of cookies done. I left you a plateful of cookies," she told him, not meeting his eyes. "Ready if you are, Tess."

"See you later," he said. He'd be back after he got his chores done.

In a whirlwind of movement and chatter, the kids went out the door. The women followed.

He stood rooted, feeling no inclination to get to work. Running his fingers through his still-damp hair, he stared across the room and through the long window beside the door. He caught sight of Dana as she walked past it. They had only a pane of glass between them, but so much more to keep them apart.

Clarice sure as hell had made certain to remind him of that.

Chapter Eleven

After lunch, Dana told Tess she'd buy ice cream for everyone. She was relieved when her offer was accepted. Her budget could stretch that far, at least.

Besides, she knew P.J. would savor his vanilla scoop in tiny little spoonfuls, as always, which meant she could delay going back to the house. Back to facing Ben and her memories of the conversation with Clarice.

Afterward, still not ready to go home, she suggested to Tess that they take a stroll along Signal Street.

Ahead of them, Lissa and Nate led the procession, with P.J. tagging behind, trying to listen in on their conversation.

"It will be nice when the playground's ready for the kids," Tess said.

"Hmm…"

"Dana, is everything all right?"

Surprised, she glanced sideways. "Yes, fine."

Tess's eyes narrowed. "Now, why do I doubt that?"

"Because you're imagining things?"

"I don't think so. You didn't even hear what I just said. And you didn't say a word when I was talking to Ben earlier. Are you upset that Caleb offered to pay for the monument?"

"No, of course not. Why would that upset me?"

"I don't know. Flagman's Folly has never done anything like this before, and everyone's so excited about the memorial." She paused, then said softly, "They're all so proud of how you're handling things on your own, too."

Dana stopped to watch P.J. run up the steps of Town Hall.

"Listen," Tess said, "it's just the two of us here now. I know there's something bothering you. You were fine yesterday, and only one thing has changed since then." She took a deep breath and let it out slowly. "If it's not Caleb, then are you upset because I'm on the monument committee?"

"Now you're being ridiculous."

At Tess's expression of relief, she tried not to cringe. She had meant what she said—of anyone in town, she'd have chosen her best friend to work on any project concerning her own family.

Except *this* project.

It wasn't Tess's participation on the committee that bothered her, but the fact that the committee existed at all.

"Talk to me, girl," Tess persisted.

Dana adjusted the light blanket over Stacey's legs. A useless delaying action because no one was going to come along to save her. And right now, she wanted that—no matter how many times she'd insisted to Ben that she could handle things herself.

She pushed the stroller forward again and sighed. The kids had taken off again. She couldn't use them for a distraction.

Her luck had finally run out.

Then she met Tess's stare and recognized the uncertainty in her best friend's face. For that reason alone, she had to talk. Not about Paul. She couldn't, especially after what had happened with Clarice. But she needed to ease Tess's worry—and badly needed to confide in her about Ben.

She and Tess and Ben and Paul had all grown up together. Had known each other forever. If anyone could help her with this situation, Tess could.

"I wasn't very open with you when Caleb came back to town—" Tess began.

She shook her head. "That's not it at all, believe me."

"All right, then what *is* it?"

After a long, deep breath, she muttered, "It's Ben."

Tess gasped. "He's objecting to the monument?"

"No, it's nothing to do with that. It's… He's taken over my life." She tried to smile. "Or at least, it feels that way. It was bad enough when he just owned the office building. Now that he's bought the house, too, he shows up almost every day. Every time I turn around, he's there."

"He's being helpful. That's just Ben."

She could have screamed. How could she expect Ella-mae and Clarice to back off, when her best friend felt the way they did? "I *know* that's just Ben. And he's very helpful. But he wants to do things for me—things I can do for myself—and it's getting on my nerves."

"It's that bad?"

"It's worse."

They walked for a few yards, then Tess said softly, "You know, I would feel lost if something ever happened to you."

Dana stared in surprise. "Same here. You know that."

"Well, then. Ben and Paul got to be best buddies back in kindergarten, just as you and I did. He probably feels lost now. Maybe he's trying to stay close to Paul through you and the kids."

She gripped the stroller. "I never thought of that."

"And you know how most guys are when it comes to talking."

"Not Ben. He's never had a problem with talking about anything."

"Except his feelings." Tess's voice rose. "I'm sure that's it. He's been quiet—different—for months now. I think you need to talk to him."

She clutched the handle with such force, her knuckles turned white. "Talk to him?" That's just what she wanted to avoid.

"Yes. Get him to tell you what's on his mind. That way, he'll start opening up."

"You could be right—" she began. *But I'll never know.*

Tess nodded emphatically. "I'm sure I am." She sighed in obvious relief at having come up with an idea that would help.

Dana tried not to cry in frustration. She should never have said anything, never have gotten Tess involved at all. Her suggestion *didn't* help. It only made things worse.

She had no intention of talking about Paul. And no desire for any heart-to-heart conversations with Ben.

But now that she had gotten Tess involved, now that Tess believed her suggestion had been accepted, she would want to know how things were going. She would expect to hear progress reports. She would be eager to learn what Dana had done to help their good old friend Ben.

ALL TOO SOON, P.J. FINISHED his ice cream and Tess drove them home.

As P.J. and Lissa climbed out of the backseat, Dana cradled Stacey in one arm. She handed Lissa the baby's car seat. "I'll see you in the office on Monday," she said to Tess. "Good luck with Jared tomorrow."

"Okay. And good luck with…you-know-who." Tess smiled.

"Thanks." Dana closed the passenger door and waved goodbye.

"Ben's truck is here again," Lissa pointed out.

She'd already noticed that. "Yes, I see it."

At that moment, the front door opened. Ben stepped out onto the porch as if he'd been lying in wait. Desire ran

through her, followed by a breath-stealing surge of awareness. No getting away from it. Good old Ben was a good-
looking guy.

After working in the yard that morning, he'd changed
into a snug, soft green T-shirt that accentuated his muscles and played up his dark hair and eyes. Before lunch,
she had walked into the living room and seen him standing there with the moisture from his shower—that shower
she'd fantasized over—still dampening his hair. Her reaction to the sight had made her ten times more eager to accept Tess's invitation.

But now she was home, and there he stood again, looking
as good as any hero from the romance novels she read. And
leaning against the porch railing as if he owned the place.
Now, annoyance mixed with desire until she reminded herself he *did* own this property and there wasn't much she
could do about it.

"Did you have a good lunch?" he asked.

"We sure did," P.J. said. "And we went for ice cream."

"Yeah? Where's mine?"

"We didn't bring you any." Lissa's glance flew to Dana
and then away.

Was she upset about finding Ben here again? Or that
they'd left him out of their plans?

Dana still wasn't sure what impact his absence had had
on her children. Or whether it had been wise for her to let
him back into their lives. As *she* couldn't decide, it was no
wonder if Lissa felt confused, too.

He shrugged. "Well, then, I guess it's only fair I ate up
all the spice cookies."

"You *did?*" P.J. gasped, and raced past him into the
house.

Lissa stared at Ben. "You didn't really, did you?"

"No, not really."

Dana followed her into the living room. "Lissa, you *do* know Ben was just teasing. He wouldn't do something like that."

She shrugged. "But...but *P.J.* didn't know that."

"That's true." And worse, she probably shouldn't have jumped to Ben's defense. Too late, she bit her tongue, thinking of the irony. Like Tess, she had fallen back on the old standard phrase, on the townsfolk's common cry: *that's just Ben.*

"Daddy wouldn't tease me or P.J. about the cookies." Frowning, she went up the stairs.

Resting her chin on the baby's head, Dana watched her go.

Ben stepped into the house and closed the screen door. She couldn't tell by his expression if he had heard Lissa's comment.

P.J. ran toward them from the kitchen. "You did *not* eat all the cookies!" he exclaimed. "Mama, can I have some?"

"Oh, I don't think so, young man. You just had a taco, tortilla chips and a dish of ice cream. That's enough for now."

He frowned but nodded. "Can we have some after supper, though?"

She tried to hold the kids to one sweet a day. But rules were meant to be broken—once in a while. "Yes, that will work."

"You gotta wait till after supper," he told Ben.

"No problem. I can do that."

She turned and stared at him. "I'm sorry, but...weren't you planning to go home before then?"

He rubbed the back of his head. "Well, to tell you the truth, I had every intention of it. But I heard how your washer sounded this morning, so I came back here and tore it to pieces."

"You didn't."

"I sure did."

She fought back a groan. The evenings she'd spent away from home this week, trying to avoid him, had forced her to do something she would never usually do. Let the laundry pile up.

Mentally, she began running through a list of all the wash she needed to get done, including the outfit she'd dug from the depths of her closet to wear to the meeting on Monday night. She needed her washing machine—in one piece.

"Good thing I took it apart, too," he said. "Left any longer, you might've needed a whole new tub. I'll have to go pick up a few parts. Judging by the pile of baskets next to the washer, I reckon you'll want it together again by tomorrow. Otherwise, it'll have to wait until Tuesday."

"Tuesday!"

He nodded. "Town council meeting on Monday. So I thought I'd keep working on it tonight."

"Good idea," she said faintly.

"That's what I thought." He turned to P.J. "Hey, buddy, how about we take a ride to the hardware store later, and then pick up a pizza for supper?"

"Yeah!" P.J. yelled.

"There's no need for that," she said. "I've got homemade soup thawing in the refrigerator. Unless you've already eaten it all?" The words, spoken half-jokingly, made her stop and think.

He laughed. "No, I didn't touch anything in the refrigerator."

"What *did* you have for lunch, anyway?"

"Not a thing. Not even that plateful of cookies you left me. I came right back and got busy wrestling with the washing machine so I could find out what it needed."

Nothing like piling on the guilt. But she couldn't complain. A serviceman would cost a small fortune. At least Ben had offered to make the repairs. She would pay for the parts.

"I'll pick up the pizza," he insisted. "It's the least I can do. After all, you fed me breakfast this morning. Besides—" he grinned "—I'm already invited for dessert."

AFTER SUPPER, BEN TOOK P.J. up on his request to read him a bedtime story while Dana put Stacey to bed and Lissa closeted herself in her bedroom.

Earlier that evening, Dana had made a big green salad and set out all kinds of vegetables to go along with their pizza. Seeing the food on the table had almost made him feel guilty for deliberately tearing her washer apart.

Almost. After all, the machine *had* made an awful racket the last time he'd heard her using it. And he hadn't been kidding about the condition of the tub.

But most of all, fool that he was, he hadn't been able to pass up the excuse to hang around tonight.

Now, while he tinkered in the utility room, she worked not five feet away from him, washing dishes.

"P.J. sure called it right about those cookies," he said. "They were great. Better than any store-bought ones. Maybe you ought to go into business." Eyeing her over the washer, he saw a small smile touch her lips.

"Thanks, but I have a career. I'll keep the cookies for my kids. I don't bake for them often enough as it is."

Because she had that career. Because she didn't have a husband and had to take care of everything herself.

"Maybe that's not so bad," she continued. "You know what they say about too much of a good thing. And I could say the same about take-out food. We don't do that very often, either."

Because she was a good mama who wanted to make

home-cooked meals for her family. And because she didn't have the money.

"The tacos last week. The pizza tonight." She looked over at him. "Those were real treats for them. Thank you."

At the sight of her smile—now wide and full and directed right at him—he nearly lost his grip on the wrench in his hand. He hadn't bought that food to earn her thanks. Or even to impress her. But if it would get him a reaction like that again, he'd clean out Harley's General Store to fill her kitchen cabinets.

Knowing he had to watch his own response to keep from scaring her away, he simply shrugged. "My pleasure. Nice for me, too, to have supper with you all now that my parents have gone."

"You must miss them." She stared down into the dishwater.

Damn. What a stupid thing he'd said. His parents had "gone" when they'd retired to Florida. A big difference from Dana, whose husband had died.

Again he wondered if he'd misjudged her over the memorial for Paul. Over the feelings she tried bravely not to let show.

He bore down so hard, the wrench slipped and flew from his hand. It went clattering into the space between the washer and the wall.

"Dang."

"Can you reach it?"

"I'm checking." He leaned over the machine and thrust his arm as far down as he could behind it. "I'll never get it without moving the washer. And I just leveled it off again."

"Maybe I can try?"

She came to his side and wiped her hands on a dish towel. Dropping the cloth on top of the dryer, she put her hands flat on the washer as if planning to boost herself up.

"You won't be able to get to it, either," he said.

"Is that so? Isn't that what you told me when your favorite marble rolled behind the bookcase in the school library?"

"Well...maybe." He grinned.

"Maybe nothing, mister." She laughed. "I saved your butt that day and you know it. Mrs. Freylin would've had a fit if she'd seen you trying to tip those shelves."

"Okay, okay. I admit, you saved me. But that was a long time ago. Your arms were thinner then."

"And they're still not as big as yours. I can probably—" She stopped.

He had reached out to keep her from climbing onto the washer. His fingers easily encircled her wrist. Her skin was firm yet soft, warm to his touch and still damp from the dishwater. Slowly he ran his thumb over the inside of her wrist, brushing away the moisture.

Her arm trembled against his fingers. Or maybe the tremor had gone through him.

No laughter. No smiles.

She looked away and took a breath so deep, her chest rose beneath her sleeveless blouse. She'd left the top two buttons undone, and in the shadows beneath the fabric he could see more soft, pale skin.

For sure now, his hands shook as he fought the urge to reach up and run his fingertip down into that deep V. But, damn—he wanted more than that. Not just the chance to touch her there. Not just her body, either.

He wanted *her*. He always had.

He reached up. Tilted his head down. And froze at the sight of her expression.

A split-second later he dropped his hand. "Dana, I—"

"No. Don't say it. Don't even think it. I'm sorry." She rushed from the utility room and through the kitchen.

He stood there, unable to believe what he had come

so close to doing. Unwilling to admit the risk he wanted to take.

And damned unhappy to realize he'd caused that stunned look on her face.

Chapter Twelve

Dana held back a sigh of exasperation and despair. How could things keep going from bad to worse?

Last night Ben had tracked her down in the living room to let her know he needed another part for the washer. He had told her he would be back before noon today. And he'd assured her—more emphatically than she wanted to recall—that what had happened wouldn't get in the way of their friendship.

Then he had left. In a hurry.

How could she blame him, after that moment in the utility room when he'd caught her staring at him? Ogling him the way Lissa and her friends ogled Jared Hall—and Caleb, before he'd become simply Nate's daddy. And then, just as Ben had started to kiss, she had run away.

With the mixed messages she kept sending, it almost wouldn't have surprised her if he hadn't come back today.

Almost, because of course, he would. He was Ben. He would never back down after he'd given someone his word.

She needed to prep meals for the week but couldn't bear the thought of working alone with him in the utility room, just a few feet away. So she'd tempted the kids into the kitchen with more cookies.

Nothing had gone right this morning. Nothing had gone right in her life for a while. Her children didn't provide the distraction she'd hoped for. Her next-door neighbor had the best intentions, Dana knew that, and the truth in those accusations had crushed her. And Ben—good old Ben—still tempted her…with something even sweeter than cookies.

He came into the kitchen now as if her thoughts had brought him to her. As she pulled the first trays out of the oven, he moved to her side. "Smells good."

"Yes. How's the washer coming along?" she asked pointedly.

"Nothing to worry about. Got that all under control." He gestured toward the trays. "You planning any extras for me?"

"Ben," she said under her breath, "you're as bad as P.J. was when Tess invited us for lunch yesterday. You know you're supposed to wait until you're asked."

"Huh. If that's the case, I could be waiting an awfully long time."

She looked up, but he had walked over to P.J. and Lissa. Biting her lip, she turned back to the trays. It had been a long time since she had invited him into their home for any reason. And to tell the truth, if he hadn't bought the house, he wouldn't be here now.

Had Tess been right? Had he waited all this time—all the months since Paul's death—for an invitation that had never come? Had he bought the house as a last resort, only so he could see more of his best friend's children?

She swallowed hard past the lump in her throat.

He and the kids sat at the table, drinking milk and eating cookies still warm from the oven. Lissa hung around watching as P.J. and Ben played a marathon card game that appeared as though it would last until noon.

Not a problem for Ben, since P.J. had already made it clear he expected him to stay for their midday Sunday dinner.

Like the roast and vegetables cooking in the pot on the back burner, mixed emotions simmered inside Dana.

P.J. had become a different little boy in these past couple of weeks, more outgoing, more easygoing, more tolerant of Lissa and her friends. She couldn't deny she owed all that to Ben.

Between that and everything else he had done around the house, she couldn't begrudge him another meal. Could she?

Those simmering emotions threatened to boil over.

At the breakfast bar, she transferred cookies from the cooling racks to her largest cookie jar. He rose from the table and came toward her.

Tensing, she tightened her hold on the spatula. She wasn't going to take the chance of having another tool slip into an inconvenient spot, the way his wrench had fallen behind the washer last night. She wasn't going to risk allowing her true feelings to show again, either.

He reached around her, attempting to grab a cookie.

Pretending playfulness she didn't feel, she pushed his arm away. "Don't you think you've had enough?"

"Well, you know how it is. You get one taste and you just want more. Besides, it's not like I get to have your homemade cookies all the time. The kids'll tell you that— right, kids?"

"Right!" Lissa and P.J. exclaimed.

She forced a laugh. "And they'll tell you just what I tell them. No more, or you'll ruin your dinner."

"That's right, too," P.J. said, not sounding nearly as enthusiastic this time.

"You see?" She shifted just as Ben reached around her again. His outstretched hand skimmed her breast.

His dark eyes held her gaze for several heartbeats.

He recovered first, dropping his hand to the counter beside her and stepping back.

Quickly, she glanced over at the kitchen table. P.J. knelt on his chair, scooping up the scattered cards, not glancing their way. Lissa sat watching them, but as her chair was on the far side of the room, she couldn't have noticed. Not that the innocent collision had meant anything, anyway.

It was just another taunting reminder of something she couldn't have.

"'Scuse me," Ben mumbled, his breath tickling her ear. As he walked toward the table, he continued in a normal tone, "Since the cookie break is over, maybe I'd best get back to work."

"You can't," P.J. said matter-of-factly. "We didn't eat supper yet. And we have to finish our game."

"Well," he said, drawing the word out, "you're right there, P.J." He dropped into his seat again. "Always a good thing to finish what you start."

Dana stared at him. Though he sat looking at P.J., had he directed his comment to her? Was he really talking about last night, telling her he wanted to be more than just friends, no matter what he had said?

But friendship was all she could give him. No matter how much she longed for more, too.

"'Finish what you start'?" she repeated brightly. "As in, finish fixing the washing machine?"

"Oh, I got that done already." He grinned.

Well, of course he had. Why tell her about it? After all, if she'd known earlier that he'd finished his job, she might have found a way to get him out of her hair—*before* P.J. had invited him to eat with them.

This time, one look told her she'd figured out exactly what he was thinking.

She covered the cookie jar and dropped the spatula into the sink. "Oh, well, thank you so much. I guess now I can go and start a load of laundry."

"You sure can," he said, taking the cards P.J. held out.

She tried not to run from the kitchen.

In the utility room a few minutes later, she braced her hands on the edge of the dryer and took a deep breath. She felt as agitated as the load of clothes she had just tossed into the washer.

Ben made her think things she shouldn't. Made her wish for things she could never have. Made her weak when she needed to be strong, for so many reasons.

And just like the clothes in the washer, her guilt and need and obligations tumbled around and around inside her.

AFTER THEIR SUNDAY DINNER, the card game started up again in the living room. Dana cleared off the kitchen table but kept her ears half tuned to the conversation.

"Can we play all day?" P.J. asked Ben.

"I doubt that. We've still got work to do outside."

"Daddy played cards with me *all* the time," Lissa said with more than a trace of smugness.

Sensing trouble, Dana edged toward the doorway.

"My daddy played cards with me, too," P.J. said.

"He did not."

"Yes, he did."

Over their heads, Ben's gaze met Dana's.

"No, he didn't," Lissa insisted. "And besides, you were too little when he was here."

"I was not—"

"You don't even remember him."

"Yes, I do." As if to prove his point, P.J. reached into his shorts pocket and held up the small photograph of Paul that he kept by his bedside. He slapped the photo on the coffee table. It was crumpled around the edges, as if he'd carried it since he'd brought it down to the kitchen yesterday. "*That's* my daddy. He's a hero."

"*You* only know that because I told you!"

"Lissa!" Dana said. "P.J. Both of you, stop."

"But P.J. doesn't know—"

"Lots of people know your daddy's a hero." Ben's voice cut across her words quietly but with such emphasis Lissa and P.J. snapped their mouths shut. "P.J. could have heard it from them. And he definitely heard it from me. Your daddy's a hero. That's why he's wearing those medals in that picture. He's an army hero."

"I know that," Lissa said.

He smiled. "There's something I'll bet you don't know. He was a hero in Flagman's Folly, too."

"He was?"

"Yep. The greatest hero the high school football team ever had. He led them to three state championships in a row. Nobody had ever done that before, and they've never done it since."

"*Wow.* Mama never told us *that.*"

Ben nodded, in agreement with her or confirmation of his own statement, Dana didn't know.

Like a dark cloud, silence hung over the room. Or over her.

"Your daddy and I were friends for a long, long time," Ben said. "Your daddy and mama and I have all been friends since we were in kindergarten."

"Like me?"

Dana didn't have to look to know her son's eyes had widened in astonishment. She wished she didn't have to listen to Ben's response. Yet she couldn't force herself to step away.

"Yes, like you. Your daddy and I were best buddies ever since then. And nothing will ever change that."

Buddies. *Friends.*

Just as they were.

"Best friends do everything together," Lissa said, "like me and Nate."

"Yep," he agreed, "just like the two of you. In fact, your daddy and I used to have sleepovers, too. Until the time we let my garter snakes loose in the house."

"In the *house?*" Lissa screeched.

Again, Dana didn't have to look to know P.J. would have just the opposite reaction. "You had *snakes!*"

"Well, I sure didn't have them for very long after that. My mama feels the way your mama does. She doesn't like 'em a bit."

"Ben," Dana said warningly, "don't give him any ideas."

He laughed. "I'm not."

Turning away, she went to Stacey and lifted her from the high chair. She wrapped her arms around the baby and rested her cheek against her hair.

Maybe she *had* been wrong about having Ben spend so much time with Lissa and P.J. The expression on her older daughter's face said she still wasn't sure how she felt about Ben. P.J.'s feelings, on the other hand, had been evident in the way he looked up adoringly at the man.

Life had gotten so complicated in the past few weeks.

No. Life had become complicated long before Paul had died. When she'd started weaving that web of deceit.

Dana tightened her hold on Stacey and the little girl squirmed. She rocked her gently and looked down at the baby she loved, the baby she had conceived in a mistaken effort to save her marriage.

She would never regret having Stacey. Still, she knew what her last-born child represented to the townsfolk of Flagman's Folly—and to Ben Sawyer. Her baby gave them additional proof of Dana's perfect marriage.

And gave her yet one more secret to hang on to.

WITH EVERY STORY HE TOLD about Paul, Ben felt worse than ever. How could he have thought about trying to get anywhere with his best friend's wife?

Clarice had blasted him with her opinion about that.

Dana herself had told him to back off the night of the wedding. And she hadn't changed her mind. He'd seen that in her face just before she'd run from the utility room. The sight had stayed with him all night, and he hadn't shaken it yet.

But he'd had years to learn how to cover his feelings.

"Hey, buddy," he said easily to P.J., "we've got a job to do. How about you run upstairs and get into some work clothes."

"Okay." The boy took off.

Lissa hadn't said much while he was telling his stories, but she didn't seem to want to miss one of them. She sat now on the edge of an ottoman and rubbed at the carpet with the toe of her shoe. He waited, thinking again of how little she resembled her mama as far as jumping into a conversation. But she'd speak up when she got good and ready.

He looked toward the kitchen. Again, Dana stood in the doorway, this time holding Stacey. In an instant, his jaw tightened.

If her reaction last night hadn't told him all he needed to know about ever having a relationship with her, seeing her hugging the baby sure as heck did. Like P.J. keeping track of tacos on his fingers, he could count back the months. He wouldn't have to go very far to know Paul and Dana had conceived that baby when Paul had come home for his last leave.

"Ben?"

He tore his gaze away and looked at Lissa. "Yeah?"

She stared back. "You were *always* best friends with Daddy?"

He nodded. "In grade school and junior high, and all through high school, too. And I was best man at his wedding."

"What's a best man?"

"When a man gets married, he's called the groom—"

"I know that. Like Caleb. And Tess was the bride."

"Exactly. The groom's best friend is called the best man, and he gets to help the groom."

"You mean, like Becky's daddy did?"

"Yes. The best man stands by the groom in church and holds the wedding ring until the groom puts it on the bride's finger."

"Oh." She sounded relieved. "Then, the best man doesn't get married."

"Well...no. Not when he's helping the groom."

"That's good." She dragged her toe across the carpet again. "Mama says you come here all the time again now because you bought this house and you need to fix it up."

The abrupt change in subject made him want to shake his head in confusion. But he didn't. Obviously, she had something in *her* head and knew where she was going with it. "Yeah, there's a lot that needs to be done around here."

She nodded. "I know. And now Daddy's gone, you're helping Mama. Like a best man, right?"

"That's right. I want to help all of you."

"Good. But you won't have to go to church to help Mama. Because she won't get married again."

He swallowed hard and told himself not to look over toward the kitchen. "She won't?"

"No."

He couldn't stop himself. When his gaze shot to the doorway, he knew Dana hadn't missed a word. She stood frozen, almost the way she had last night.

Before she had run from him.

He forced himself to focus again on Lissa, who sat shaking her head.

"Miss Clarice says *she* can't get married again, because Mr. Vernon was a hero. And she says nobody can take Daddy's place because he's a hero, too."

"She's right. He sure is." He hesitated, then said, "Is that what's got you all quiet with me lately? You're thinking I'm trying to replace your daddy?"

She shrugged and nodded. "Yeah."

"Well, don't worry about that at all. I told you, I was his best friend. And I'm here to help out."

She nodded. "Now you told me. Because you're Mama's best man." She looked over toward the kitchen. "Right, Mama?"

Ben looked that way again, too.

"Right," Dana said.

Smiling now, Lissa went upstairs.

Dana had disappeared from the doorway.

He sat there for a moment or two, but when it became clear she didn't intend to return, he got up and ambled into the kitchen. She stood leaning against the breakfast bar, her arms still wrapped around Stacey. When she saw him, she seemed to stiffen, but he didn't let it deter him. He headed directly across the room and came to a stop just in front of her.

"Is that what you're worried about, too?" he asked. "That I'm here trying to take over? Trying to replace Paul?"

She shook her head.

"Well, just in case, you heard what I said to Lissa. I'm here to help you and the kids."

"Yes, I know. You've said that all along."

"And you've never been happy about it. I can't say I understand that." He took a long, calming breath and reached up to stroke Stacey's hair lightly with one finger. Trying to keep his voice just as gentle, he said, "You know, these are Paul's kids, too. No matter how you and I feel about everything, maybe we ought to consider what he would have wanted."

DANA RESTED HER CHIN in her hands and stared down at the tabletop without seeing it. A while ago, Ben and P.J. had left the house to go out into the yard to work. Lissa had gone onto the back porch with a book.

When Ben had started telling his stories, she had wanted to sink into a puddle and melt into the floor. Like the Wicked Witch of the West in the kids' favorite movie.

Oh—and wasn't that an appropriate comparison! Because she felt wicked. She felt awful. She felt racked with guilt and more. Clarice had seen right through her.

Wanting her husband's best friend made her ashamed.

Ben was so wrong about expecting her to take Paul's thoughts into consideration, though she could never tell him that.

Yet he was so right about everything else.

If she ever again lost herself in daydreams, no doubt he would be the first to remind her they could never come true.

And everyone in Flagman's Folly would back him up.

"Mama!" Lissa yelled from the porch. "P.J.'s hurt!"

Dana jumped to her feet. After a quick glance at Stacey, safely strapped into her high chair, she rushed across the room.

Outside, Lissa stood pointing to the opposite end of the yard. "He fell into the hole where Ben was digging, but Ben already saved him."

Even from this distance, she could see Ben kneeling beside her son, who stood chattering away.

"It doesn't seem like he's hurt. I'll take a look, though. Please go keep an eye on Stacey."

The screen door slapped shut behind Lissa as Dana went down the back steps. She watched Ben check out P.J.'s arms and legs under the guise of brushing loose dirt from his clothing.

"Everything all right?" Clarice had come outside, too, and rushed in their direction. "My goodness. I was looking out the window and when I saw him fall, I just—"

"Nothing to worry about," Ben interrupted. "He's fine."

He clapped his hands on P.J.'s pants legs. A dust cloud rose, sending her son into giggles.

Clarice took his hand. "Well, he may be fine, but he's filthy. He can come along with me, and I'll clean him up a bit. And then maybe he'll help me make a dent in a gallon of ice cream taking up space in my freezer. How about that, P.J.?"

"Sure, Miss Clarice. I can do that."

Now he could think only of his treat. But without that, and given time to stop and dwell on what had happened, it wouldn't have taken much to send him into tears. And he did seem fine. Grateful for her neighbor's quick thinking, Dana mouthed a "thank you" to Clarice.

The older woman nodded stiffly. She hadn't forgotten their conversation. Or forgiven. But at least she wasn't taking her feelings out on the kids.

As she led P.J. away, he grinned and gave Dana a big wave. She waved back. Then, forcing a smile, she turned to Ben, who looked more upset than P.J. had right after his fall. "None the worse for wear."

He finished dusting himself off and shook his head. "I'm glad for that. Scared the hell out of me when I saw him slip. He was too far away for me to catch him."

"He's quick. And with all the time he's spent with you lately, I'm just amazed you haven't seen him take a spill before now."

"You sound like you expected it."

"It's more like I'm used to it. You remember, he had those stitches from falling off the coffee table when he was three."

"Yeah, I do remember. I guess he's a typical boy, huh?"

She laughed. "Nothing's typical when it comes to kids. Girls get into just as many scrapes. Lissa has had her share of bumps and bruises. And at the rate she's going, I'm sure Stacey will, too."

"It's a lot to deal with, isn't it? A big responsibility, watching over kids."

"So, you've noticed." She'd said the words with a hint of irony, but the fact that he *had* noticed pleased her. Maybe now he would give her some credit. Would accept the fact that she could take care of her kids.

"I never realized it involved so much worry," he said. "And so much work. Especially with three of them."

"It can be challenging. They're a handful at times."

"I see that." He shook his head. "And here you've been dealing with this on your own. I told you I'm here to help. You can depend on that, doubled. Or maybe I should say tripled. I'll make it a point to stop in as much as I can."

Here we go again. It was all she could do not to snap at him. "Ben, I appreciate that, thank you. But—"

"No thanks necessary," he interrupted. "Maybe you have managed all right alone. Now you don't have to." He stared her down. "At least, not around *this* house."

Obviously, he'd set his mind on that. And now he'd set his jaw, too. Eyes glittering, he stood taller and looked even more determined.

And very, very sexy.

She backed up a step, shaking her head, whether in response to her thoughts or his words, she couldn't tell.

"I'm going to pack it in for the day," he said. "I'll be seeing you tomorrow—"

"I don't think so—"

"—at the town council meeting," he finished without missing a beat.

"Oh, right." How could she have forgotten?

She couldn't think around him. And obviously couldn't convince him of anything.

She'd better have her head on straight tomorrow night. She and Kayla had so many dreams for the kids of Flagman's Folly wrapped up in the proposal they planned to present.

She could only hope that, unlike Ben, the rest of the council would listen to reason.

Chapter Thirteen

"We believe Flagman's Folly should provide a common area for children to play in, such as the one we propose."

Dana stood at the small podium reserved for anyone who wanted speak at a town council meeting. She tried to put her conviction into her words as she addressed the men and women seated at the long conference table at the front of the room. Behind them loomed Judge Baylor's massive wooden bench, the focal point of the courtroom adding solemnity to the occasion.

She swallowed hard and continued, "We also believe the children would benefit greatly from this playground. In addition—"

At the sight of several heads nodding even before she had finished her speech, she shot a triumphant glance in Kayla's direction—and promptly came to a halt when she saw the look on her friend's face. Something was wrong.

They had arrived late to the meeting. At the first break, she and Kayla had squeezed into the only seats left available, on the end of the front row beside Tess and Caleb Cantrell.

Kayla and Tess both sat staring at her in dismay. From the row behind them, Ellamae whispered into their ears.

"Dana?" Ben asked. "Are you with us?"

Quickly she turned her attention back to the council.

Ben was the chairman, but so far she had managed to meet everyone's gaze but his. "Yes," she replied, still not looking at him. "As I started to say, in addition, based on the facts we've outlined, we propose the council allocate the lot northwest of the elementary school for the playground."

Now the whispers came from all around the courtroom.

Now a few of the council members looked dismayed, too. Not one of them would look her way—except Ben. She refused to meet his gaze.

"Excuse me." Ellamae rose from her seat and hurried to stand beside Dana at the podium. "Since Dana and Kayla missed the earlier proceedings tonight—"

"They had car trouble, Ellamae. They explained that." Council member Joe Harley, also owner of the general store on Signal Street, smiled at Dana.

She winced. The new battery had done its job, but something else inside her van had quit on their way to Town Hall. They'd had to push the van to the curb with some help from a couple of teenagers and then hurry on foot the rest of the way.

"I know the details," Ellamae said with exaggerated patience. "I was here helping to present the *other* proposal on tonight's agenda. Remember?"

As the town clerk, Ellamae felt as comfortable speaking her mind in this courtroom as she did anywhere else in town. It didn't help that she'd known Dana and Joe since they were born.

She turned to Dana. "Tess doesn't want to break this news to you, and you couldn't have been aware of it, of course, seeing as you weren't here—" she glanced at Joe "—due to your aforementioned trouble with your vehicle. But we already presented our proposal for the memorial for Paul."

Dana nodded stiffly. "I assumed that's what you meant."

"And the monument's going on that very plot of land near the school."

Dana's heart sank. She turned to the front of the room. "But that location's the only property available that—"

Ben held up his hand, cutting her off, and now she had no choice but to meet his eyes. He looked as determined as he had the day before. And yes, just as sexy.

He also looked annoyed.

"Hold on a minute," he said. But his annoyance didn't seem to be directed toward her. He had turned his attention to Ellamae. "Your proposal—your very *worthwhile* proposal—was presented. But the council hasn't voted on it yet."

"What does that matter? Ben Sawyer, you know darn well it *will* be approved."

"Not tonight, it won't. We'll table discussion on both proposals until the next meeting."

"Thinks he's the judge here," she muttered, low enough that only Dana overheard.

"Excuse me?" Ben said.

She grinned. "You're in charge here."

"Right. Then, as we've come to the last item on our agenda, I'll call this meeting adjourned."

His eyes narrowed, and the look of intense irritation on his face made Dana's pulse skip a beat. This time it wasn't directed at Ellamae, but at her.

She hurried to follow the folks streaming through the double doors. Outside, Caleb moved ahead through the crowd, but Kayla and Tess stopped off to one side of the doorway to wait for her.

As soon as she reached them, Tess said, "If I'd had any idea we had chosen the same site for both proposals, I would have tried to suggest some other location to our committee."

"It's just an unlucky coincidence," Kayla said.

But the site is *perfect for the playground.* Dana couldn't say that. Obviously, Tess felt terrible. "You would have had a hard time trying to sway Ellamae if she had her heart set on it, anyhow."

"She did," Tess said.

One of the people exiting the hall came to a stop by Dana's side. The scent of spice told her who it was.

"Hey, folks," Ben said. "Dana, got a minute?"

She eased a step away. "No, actually. I can't stop to chat. I promised Anne I'd come right home after the meeting."

"Then I'll give you a ride," he said, "seeing as you don't have a vehicle. No argument." He smiled. "It's on my way."

"Great," Tess said. "We're taking Kayla home—and we've got to run before we hit a traffic jam. I'll see you at the office in the morning, Dana. Night, Ben."

The two women hurried off.

She sighed. "Thanks for the offer, but it's only a couple of blocks. And please don't say anything about walking alone at night. Flagman's Folly is the safest place in the state." She watched Tess and Kayla cross the street and added under her breath, "We don't have traffic jams here, either."

"With only one traffic light on Signal Street, how could we? But that reminds me. What about your van?"

"I'll call the garage when I get home."

"Then the sooner you get there the better, before Ron closes up shop for the night."

"Not necessarily," she said sweetly. "You know everyone in town has his home phone number."

Ellamae and Roselynn emerged from the building.

"Dana!" Tess's mother exclaimed. "You're still here? Why, I wonder how come Tess and Caleb didn't take you home. Ellamae's got her car. Can we give you a lift?"

"All taken care of, ladies," Ben said. "Thanks, anyway."

"That's our Ben," Ellamae said, nodding.

Before Dana could say anything, both women beamed at him, then moved down the steps. As soon as they had gone out of earshot, she hissed, "I could have accepted and saved you the trouble."

"No trouble. I've got to pick up some tools I left at your place, anyway."

She exhaled heavily. "Ben Sawyer, remind me. Did you ever in your life lose an argument?"

He laughed. "No. And I don't aim to start."

A noisy group spilled out onto the porch, jostling her. She and Ben stepped aside.

Now that he wasn't glaring at her with irritation, as he had inside the courtroom, she noticed how the streetlamp picked up the warm tone of his brown eyes. How it highlighted the darkness and fullness of his dark lashes. Women would pay a fortune for mascara that could give them lashes like that.

In the lower lighting, his face seemed different, too. Harder. More rugged. Even more interesting with the play of shadows carving his cheeks.

She wanted to touch him. Again. Just a gentle graze of his jaw, the way his hand had accidentally brushed her breast. At those thoughts, at that memory, at the sudden darkening of his eyes, as if he might be recalling that moment, too, she started to shake inside.

"Come on," he said, his voice rough, "let's get you home."

BEN MADE THE SHORT, almost-silent trip back to Dana's house in record time. If she hadn't had to get home to tuck the kids in and call Ron at the garage, he might've pulled over to talk. As it was, he bit his tongue and focused on the road. He'd get his turn. He'd make sure of that. He wasn't going home until he'd found out the truth about that look he'd seen in her eyes just a short while ago.

A look that had finally given him hope.

When she opened the front door and went upstairs, he waited a second, then moseyed over to take a seat on the couch. Better just to wait until her sitter left. Then they wouldn't have anything or anyone to distract them.

As she and Anne came down the stairs, she took one look at him and narrowed her eyes. She'd probably expected him to leave after he'd gotten his tools…the ones he hadn't actually left behind.

Anne said good-night, and the two of them went outside.

When Dana finally came back in and closed the door, he sat waiting. Instead of crossing to the living room, she moved to peer through the long window beside the front door.

"Something interesting out there?" he asked.

"I'm just seeing that Anne and Billy get to his car."

"Why? Not twenty minutes ago, you told me this is the safest town in the state."

"I'd just like to keep an eye on them," she said without turning. "They *are* still only kids."

He walked over to her. "Is that why? Or are you putting off talking to me, the way you did in the truck on the way home?"

"That's ridiculous."

Gently he took her by the arm and turned her to face him. "Is it? Or are you afraid?"

"Afraid? Of you?"

He might've taken offense at her scathing tone, except her laugh sounded forced. She didn't plan to make this easy for him. Maybe it wasn't easy on her, either. But he had to know if he'd really understood what he'd seen in her eyes.

"Now," he said softly, "who's talking trash? You'll never

have anything to fear from me, and we both know that. You're afraid of what you were thinking outside Town Hall."

She shook her head. "Ben, I hate to tell you this. You can't read minds."

"I can read eyes, though. And faces. Especially yours, since I've known you so long. Take right now. I'm reading annoyance, clear as anything."

She groaned. "Okay, I'll grant you that. At the moment, anyone in the world could see it." She sighed heavily. "You know, we seem to do this all the time. We're as bad as Lissa and P.J., bickering like a couple of kids."

"That's just what I'm getting at. We're adults, not kids." He slid his hand from her arm to her shoulder. "We can stop bickering all on our own."

She shook her head again, as if in pity. But beneath his palm, she trembled. "Somehow I doubt that."

"You know better. And you've known me just as long as I've known you." He held his breath, contemplating what he would do next. The action could ruin that friendship forever. But no matter what she said, no matter the look on her face the other night when they'd stood this close, he knew what he'd seen in her eyes just a while ago. He reached up and touched her cheek. "I'll bet my ranch you can read me right now, too."

"The question is," she said, her voice shaking, "why would I want to?"

He laughed softly. "I can think of a few reasons." He bent his head and touched her mouth briefly with his. So briefly that if he'd closed his eyes first, he might have missed it.

Her eyes went wild, like those of a colt he was trying to break, and again, like a colt, she reared. Her back hit the door behind her with a thud.

"No," she said, crossing her arms. "We can't do this. Didn't those run-ins with Clarice tell you that?" She sighed.

"I'm sorry. There have been a lot of mixed messages and crossed signals being sent around here lately. But that won't happen again. I promise you."

Those last words chilled him as effectively as a plunge into Sidewinder Creek in midwinter. Made him see sense just as effectively. He took a step back and nodded. "Yeah, you're right. It won't happen again."

"We *are* friends. But that's all. Right?"

He heard the desperation in her voice, as if nothing in the world meant more to her than having him agree.

He could almost see them again at their kindergarten desks. Him. Dana. And Paul.

"Right." He took a long, deep breath and let it out. "I'm your friend. And honorary uncle to your kids. Then, of course, there's our business relationship. I own the house. You pay the rent. And we can't forget our other relationship."

She hesitated. "What other relationship?"

"I'm on the council, and I hold the deciding vote. You presented a proposal. Right?" he pressed, just as she had done a moment ago.

"Right." She shook her head ruefully. "That was a real coincidence, two proposals involving the same property. But the site's perfect for—"

He held up his hand, just as he had in the courtroom. "You had plenty of chances to talk to me before tonight. You didn't want my help. No sense trying to convince me now." He couldn't keep the bitterness from his tone. No matter how much his feelings for her tied his thoughts up in knots, his mind stayed clear on one thing.

She refused to honor Paul.

"You could be right about the site for the playground. But why isn't it an equally good place for the tribute to your husband?" He'd kept his voice low, yet she flinched as if he'd shouted the question at her. "And why is it, all along, you haven't supported the idea of that memorial?"

"That's *my* business." Her eyes flashed. "And it's got nothing to do with any of *our* relationships." She stepped aside. "Excuse me. I have to call about my van. You shouldn't have any trouble finding your way out, since you're a foot away from the door."

She moved past him and hurried to the stairs, leaving him standing there looking after her. Leaving him angry. Sick. And disgusted with himself.

The way he had felt for days now.

He didn't understand why she wouldn't accept the idea of the monument. Why she still refused to honor Paul. But hadn't he done the same—no, hadn't he done much worse—by lusting after his best friend's widow?

No matter how much he wanted Dana, even with the ghost of his best friend standing between them, he couldn't disrespect her by going against her wishes. Not even for the pleasure of a one-night stand.

Not that she'd give him that now.

And if she ever did, he'd have his one night in paradise, that's all. Because the next morning, she'd regret it, and that would be the end. Of everything.

She'd never take him on as a long-term lover. She might reject him even as a friend. He couldn't run that risk.

He needed her.

Chapter Fourteen

Ben fiddled with the handle of his coffee mug, debating whether he should ask Dori for another fill-up.

Monday night, after the town council meeting and their talk at her house, he'd let Dana kick him out. He'd gone slinking off like a mutt with its tail between its legs—because he hadn't known what to say. A hell of a thing to admit, for a man who almost always had the last word.

He'd stayed away from her place yesterday. Tough to do, since he missed seeing the kids. But he fought against stopping by. He didn't want to run into her. Yet.

In the long run, the distance had done him good because he'd had time to figure things out. In all these months since Paul had died, he'd done his best to get close to her, trying to help her. Trying to make her his.

And in these few short days, he'd discovered he'd done every damn-fool thing possible.

"Coffee, Ben?"

He looked up at Dori and nodded. "Last one. Then I'll be getting out of your way."

"What is that, 'get out of my way'? You are always welcome at the Double S." She smiled as she topped up his mug. "It's good to have you visit us for supper again."

He'd come in with a couple of his ranch hands, who had left afterward to go have a few beers. Now he'd hung around so long, he'd outstayed all the other diners. But he hadn't worn out his welcome here, the way he had with Dana.

As if she'd read his thoughts, Dori said, "Tess and Dana came in this afternoon with their new client. That big rodeo man, what's his name?"

No use pretending he didn't know. He'd heard it often enough around Dana's house. "Jared Hall."

"Yes. They hope they will make a sale to him." She went back to the kitchen, leaving him with his coffee.

Yeah, as if he didn't have enough to think about, there was Jared Hall. Like Caleb Cantrell, another big rodeo star. Unlike Caleb, a man who'd caught Dana's eye. And maybe not just for the commission.

He scowled down at his coffee mug. Then he shook his head, knowing he was avoiding the man he needed to think about.

Paul.

He pushed his mug aside and dropped some bills on the table. They'd settled his check earlier so Dori could close up the cash register.

After a quick good-night, he went out to his truck and decided to swing past Dana's before heading to the ranch. As he'd told her the other night, it was on his way home.

After ten o'clock now, and the shops had long ago rolled up their sidewalks. The temperature had dropped below average for the month, and most folks had their doors and windows closed, too. But at Dana's, the front door stood open. A rectangle of light fell across the porch and down the steps to the sidewalk.

He frowned. As he pulled to a stop in front of the house, a figure moved in the shadows of the porch. Anne, the sitter.

She walked out to the curb. "Hi," she said. "Dana's not home yet."

"No problem. Just passing through. I saw the door open and wondered about it. Something up?"

She shook her head. "No. Dana said Billy could come by for a while because she's out so late with Mr. Hall."

Would he never get away from that name? Would Dana ever get away from the man?

"They're out on a date." She giggled. "Billy and I weren't, really, since we were just hanging out, y'know?"

Yeah, he knew. He had gone on his fair share of those kinds of dates, too. When he'd gone out with the whole gang. And sometimes, when he'd only tagged along with Paul and Dana.

"He just went around the corner. You must have passed him. I left the door open—" she jerked her thumb over her shoulder, indicating the house "—in case the baby cried. But the kids are all asleep, and Dana ought to be home soon."

"From her date," he said in a level tone.

She nodded.

In spite of his…irritation, he felt better knowing she wasn't off somewhere alone in a van that might break down.

They said good-night, and he drove on. He could've kicked himself now for driving by. He didn't need to hear the news.

Dana and Jared Hall, out on a date. Together.

The coffee he'd downed burned in his gut. But it told him what he'd been trying to ignore. Irritation, hell—he wanted to kick the man's ass for even daring to look at his girl.

And *that* told him the real reason for his bad attitude.

No matter what he'd said to himself the past few days, no matter what he tried to force himself to believe about staying friends with Dana, he couldn't do it.

That would never be enough.

Way back in kindergarten, he'd never had the nerve to

challenge his best friend for her attention. Now he no longer had to hold himself up against a man who was gone.

Now all he had to contend with was a real, live rodeo star.

He turned onto Signal Street, empty of traffic, and coasted along. He didn't plan to go by the office. They were probably out of town, anyway.

But down the block, once again, he saw lights shining across a sidewalk. Lights from the real estate office. The office in the building he owned. He kept coasting along. He ought to make sure that no one had broken into the place—even though Dana seemed to find Flagman's Folly the safest darned town in New Mexico.

He pulled to the curb and looked through the storefront window. Inside the office, she sat at her desk. Alone.

Judging by the paperwork spread out in front of her and the tape trailing from her calculator down to the floor, she'd sat there for some time.

Whatever she needed to figure, he'd give her something else to add to her calculations. He'd always been there for her, and he wasn't going anywhere now. He wasn't walking away. He wasn't losing out again. Because he was as good a man as anyone—including her rodeo star.

She'd need some time to think that over before she could accept it. He'd give her that time, no matter how long she took.

What did a few more years matter, when he'd already waited since kindergarten?

DANA SCRIBBLED ANOTHER NUMBER on her notepad and made a face at it. The total hadn't changed since the previous week. And Jared still hadn't made up his mind.

Sighing, she put down her pencil. He was an intelligent man, good at conversation, and with a face any woman would love seeing across the table at a cozy little Italian restaurant. She had loved it tonight, too, no denying that. But that's as cozy as she would get. He just wasn't the man for her.

When he'd asked for another date, she had turned him down gently, hoping it wouldn't affect his decision about buying property. Either way, she couldn't pin all her expectations on a sale to him.

After dropping him off at the Whistlestop, she should have gone home. On her quick detour to the office, the new stack of bills in the mail Tess had left on the desk distracted her.

But now, nothing could distract her from her new worries.

When she had arrived home from work yesterday, Anne never mentioned a word about Ben. Finally, she'd broken down and asked. Anne said he hadn't come by the house at all.

Frowning, she pushed the stack of papers away from her.

She ought to be grateful that he'd paid attention, for once, and had stayed away. Landlord or not, he wouldn't show up on the doorstep as often anymore. Not after Monday night. She and the kids would do better not having him around.

The sound of a tap on the office door startled her. She looked up.

Despite everything she had just told herself, when she saw who stood outside, she couldn't stop her immediate rush of pleasure. But, instantly, another instinctive response took its place.

Self-preservation.

Oh, please, not now.

Her thought didn't make Ben leave. And *she* couldn't make him leave, since he'd pulled his own key out of his pocket and unlocked the door.

As if he planned to stay a while, he took a seat next to her desk.

"Don't get comfortable on my account," she warned. "I'm about ready to pack it in."

"Yeah, I can understand that, after another late night with your client."

She opened her mouth to answer, then abruptly changed what she'd planned to say. "What makes you think I was with Jared?"

"Anne said—"

"You asked Anne?"

"Well…" He shrugged. "Yeah."

"Ben Sawyer, I thought we had this settled. You don't need to check up on me. I'm fine. The van is fine. Ron said it was only a loose connection."

His eyes widened, as if in surprise. "Is that what you think I'm here for tonight? To check up? Nope. That's got nothing to do with why I'm sitting in this chair."

"Then what is it? What are you doing here?"

"Do you really want to know?"

She sighed. "Probably not, but I'm asking."

"Jealous," he said flatly.

"What?"

"That's what I'm doing here." He slapped his palm on the desktop. "You were out and it was late and I was driven here by worry mixed with plain, damn jealousy."

She shook her head in the hope of making sense of his words. That didn't work. "Jealous of what?"

"Not what. Who. That rodeo cowboy. Now that we've got that *settled*," he emphasized, throwing her own word back at her, "need any help with that?" He gestured toward her paperwork.

This wasn't the Ben she knew. He was different tonight. But she wasn't. From now on, she couldn't allow herself to be anything but a woman protecting her secrets. Taking a deep breath, she folded her hands on the desk in front of her. "Ben."

He sat back in the chair, stretched his legs full-length and crossed them at the ankles. Staring down at his boots, he said, "You remember kindergarten?"

She blinked. He definitely was not himself, and he was mixing her up. But she wouldn't let him see that. "Yes."

"You remember how, when the timer rang, that meant we had to clean up the classroom?"

"Yes." If this was a game of Twenty Questions, she didn't plan to lose.

"Who always goofed around and made everybody laugh, but never picked up anything?"

"Paul."

"And who carried those little plastic bins around while you put the scissors and the glue sticks and the crayons into them?"

"You."

"Well, there you go." He kept his gaze focused on his boots. His dark lashes hid his eyes.

Just as well he wasn't watching her, because her eyes had begun to water. She did remember those days. And so many that came after them. Swallowing hard, she clamped her hands together.

"Telling me not to help you," he said, "is like telling Firebrand not to run. Or Becky's pup, Pirate, not to bark. Or Sidewinder Creek not to flow. Nature has to take its course. And so do I."

"Ben!" He made her crazy. But she couldn't hold back a laugh.

He grinned, still looking at his boots. "Well, it's true."

"Okay, I give in. And I'll admit it. You did help me. You helped everyone."

"That's true, too." At last, he raised his eyes to look at her, and she felt no desire to laugh. "Folks help other folks they care about, Dana." He leaned forward. "And remember, I always helped you the most." Lightly, he drew his finger across the back of her wrist.

She caught her breath, recalling the night they'd stood in her utility room and he'd held her wrist in his fingers. The night they'd kissed on the couch and he'd held her in his arms.

He stroked her hand, his finger tingling her sensitized skin. She had to fight not to lean toward him.

Just as she lost the struggle and moved forward, he sat back in his chair.

She took a deep, shaky breath, needing desperately to clear her mind. It didn't work. She had to get away from him. If he wouldn't leave, she would. Hands trembling, she shuffled her paperwork together and stowed it in her desk drawer. "Time to call it a night."

"I'll trail you home."

She looked at him.

"I'm leaving town, and it's on my way."

She hesitated, then nodded.

He followed her the few blocks to the house, where she parked the van. With the engine still running, she clung to the key ring in the ignition. He'd want to come inside with her. And she knew what he'd want next. The way he'd touched her just minutes ago told her that. Heaven help her, she wanted it, too.

Would she be able to resist?

When she walked across the yard, he stayed in his truck at the curb. Still expecting him to join her, she opened the front door. He flashed his lights and waved in farewell. Her heart gave a funny little flip, whether out of disappointment or relief, she didn't know.

She waved back, feeling cool and collected on the outside, hot and needy on the inside, and all mixed up whichever way she examined herself.

For a long time, she stood watching him drive away.

Then she closed the door and turned around and discovered Anne standing in the living room with her arms crossed.

"Where have you been all this time, young lady?" the teen asked, attempting to frown. "And who was that young man who just drove you home?"

Dana forced a laugh. "We had separate vehicles."

"A likely story." Anne's wide grin put dimples in both her cheeks. "He tracked you down, huh? I knew he would."

"He just happened to drive past the office while I was still there."

"Like I just happened to need something from Harley's every day Billy had to work?"

"No, this is different. Ben and I are just friends."

"Yeah." Anne nodded. "That's what Billy thought about us."

Dana smiled. But after Anne had gone home with her father and Dana made her way upstairs, the sitter's words came back to her, and she shook her head. Unlike Anne and Billy, she and Ben *were* just friends.

She frowned. He hadn't acted like himself at all. But no matter what crazy notion he'd gotten into his head tonight, he'd soon regret the idea.

Yet another reason for her to feel guilty for the mixed signals she kept sending.

After she'd gotten ready for bed, she made one last trip to the kids' rooms. As she tucked the dinosaur quilt around P.J., he stirred and opened his eyes.

"Mama," he whispered. "Hey, Mama…Ben didn't come for two whole days. You think he's coming tomorrow?"

She clutched the edge of the quilt. "I don't know," she said honestly.

"Maybe he will. I like Ben, Mama. I want a daddy like Ben."

He closed his eyes again and rolled over while she stood there frozen, trying to figure out what she could have said that wouldn't have broken his heart.

Or hers.

THE NEXT EVENING, with the dishwasher running and the counters cleaned, Dana felt at loose ends. Lissa sat at the kitchen table doing her homework, and P.J. had gone upstairs with his dinosaurs.

Neither of them had talked much at supper.

No one had said a word about Ben.

After helping Lissa with a couple of her English sentences, she went out to straighten the living room. A few minutes later, the doorbell rang. She stilled with her hands on the afghan she'd been folding.

Somehow, she knew she would find Ben on the doorstep.

Crossing from the living room to the entryway, she managed to take one normal breath. When she opened the door and saw what he held cradled in his arms, the small, polite smile she'd forced onto her lips slid away. "What is *that?*"

"A present."

She could hear P.J. running down the hallway upstairs. He'd be disappointed to find she'd beaten him to the door. Especially when he saw Ben there. *And* when he saw what Ben stood holding.

"Go away," she said through gritted teeth. "You can't bring that in here."

P.J.'s sneakers hit the stairs. "Who's there, Mama?"

"Come on, Dana, it's for the kids."

She shook her head and closed her eyes. Maybe she could make *everything* go away.

"Hey."

She jumped, and her eyes flew open. Ben had whispered the word against her ear. From inches away, she met his gaze. The corners of his eyes crinkled when he smiled. "It'll be okay. I promise."

No, it wouldn't. It was just another promise she couldn't let him keep.

P.J. ran up behind her. "A puppy!" he shrieked.

Ben slipped past her into the house. She closed the door and rested her head against it. Behind her, the babble rose. The high-pitched yap of the dog. Excited questions from P.J. Squawks of astonishment from Lissa, who had come running in from the kitchen.

And above it all, a deep laugh of happiness mixed with satisfaction. Ben's.

Ben couldn't have come up with a more devious plan than trying to get to her by getting *himself* in good with her kids. Somehow, she would have to harden her heart against his scheme. And pray she'd have more success with that than she'd had in trying not to obsess over him.

She turned.

Lissa and P.J. sat on the edge of the couch. Ben knelt beside the coffee table with the whimpering dog in his hands.

"It's like Christmas." Lissa sounded entranced.

Ben handed the dog to P.J., who held the wriggling bundle carefully in both arms.

Lissa leaned over to pet one of the dog's floppy ears. Big, sad brown eyes stared up at her. "What is he?" she asked.

"It's a she," Ben said. "She's just a plain old hound dog."

"We have to name her."

"Duke." P.J.'s tone said he would accept no argument.

"You can't give a girl a boy's name," Lissa argued.

"Why not? Nate's a girl, isn't she? *She's* got a boy's name. I like Duke." The dog looked at him and yipped again. P.J. nodded emphatically. "See, she likes it, too. It's a good dog's name. *Duke.*"

"No—"

"How about Duchess?" Ben asked quickly.

P.J. frowned. "What's that?"

"It's a girl duke." He turned to Lissa. "You know, like prince and princess. Duke and duchess."

"*Oh-h-h.* Yeah. I like that. Okay, P.J.?"

"Okay." He grinned. "Thanks, Ben. Thanks a lot! I always wanted a puppy." His eyes shone.

So did the dog's.

And, when Ben looked at her, so did his.

But when he started across the room toward her, she blinked back the tears that threatened and braced herself, literally, against the door.

She had to get him to take back that dog.

The minute he reached her, she spoke, her voice low so the kids wouldn't hear. But she'd bet he would have no trouble reading the anger in her eyes.

"Ben, what do you think you're doing?"

"You said you'd like to have a dog."

"Yes, I did. But I said *someday.* I can't—" She choked on the word and had to start again. "I told you, we can't have a dog. I work all day."

"Clarice said she'll keep an eye on her for you."

Wonderful. The whole town would know what he'd done. "You told Clarice about the dog?"

"Clarice and Ellamae told me. When I said I wanted a puppy for the kids, they came along to help me pick her out at the pound."

Even better. Now all of Flagman's Folly would know *she'd* turned away a poor homeless puppy. A puppy who now yelped in the background. A puppy who had just made P.J. and Lissa laugh.

How would she manage to explain this to the kids?

"I don't want a dog cooped up in the house," she said.

"Let her out in the yard."

"It's too hot in the summertime. And there's no shade."

"So I'll build a doghouse and plant a tree."

She groaned. Would he never give up? "I don't like the idea of staking a—"

He raised his brows.

She snapped her mouth shut in instant understanding. "The fence," she hissed when she could speak again. "*That's* why you put up the fence, isn't it?"

He smiled.

He means well. He always does. Take a deep breath before you blast him.

Instead, she sighed. Blasting wouldn't work. She needed to be truthful and explain her most important reason for digging in her heels. She kept her voice low but made her tone uncompromising. "We can't keep the dog." Quickly, she put her fingers to his lips to prevent him from responding. The warmth of his skin almost made her forget what she'd planned to tell him. "I can't—" Her voice broke.

He smiled again, his mouth tickling her fingertips.

She snatched her hand away. Her cheeks burned, partly from allowing him to see her reaction and the rest from knowing what she had to admit. "I can't afford to feed him," she muttered.

"Her." He kept his voice low, too. "And she comes with a lifetime supply of dog food and unlimited veterinary care."

"I can't accept that."

"Why not? We're still friends, aren't we? Just like you said the other night?"

She swallowed a sigh of both relief and disappointment.

So, they were back to that again. How quickly he'd managed to come to his senses.

With anyone else but Ben, she would have thought he'd repeated her words to hurt her. But, no, he meant them. Chances were, if she let him, he'd pay for her grocery and doctor bills, too. He only wanted to help.

She needed to remember that the next time her expression threatened to give her secrets away.

He moved closer. She could feel the heat radiating from him. Had to look up to see his eyes. Had to curl her fingers to keep them by her sides.

"Dana." His voice rumbled her name. She would swear she'd felt it vibrate through her. "Let me do this. For them. Because, like it or not, I will be here for you and your kids for the rest of my life."

Chapter Fifteen

"Have you had your talk with Ben yet?" Tess asked as they crossed the Double S parking lot.

Always busy on a Friday night, the café already had customers seated outside. Tiny lights strung around the patio twinkled like fireflies in the twilight.

Dana tried not to groan at her friend's question. She'd had plenty of talks with Ben. Too many talks. But none she could share with Tess. "No. Not yet. Jared has kept me busy."

"Well, now he's left town, he can't stop you from having your chat."

"No." She wished she could argue that point.

And when she followed Tess through the front door of the restaurant, she immediately wished she could turn around and leave. Even as the thought struck, Caleb waved at them from a booth on the opposite side of the café. Across from him, Ben turned to look and smiled.

They had held the closing for Caleb's new ranch earlier in the week, and he'd wanted to celebrate at the Double S. She hadn't realized he'd planned a party for four.

When she had walked over to the Whistlestop to drop the kids off just now and caught a ride here with Tess, her best friend hadn't said a word about Ben joining them for supper. Well, she'd give Tess the benefit of the doubt. Maybe he and Caleb had just run into each other.

Gripping her handbag with suddenly damp fingers, she took the seat beside Ben.

Caleb wrapped his arm around Tess. "Hey, Dana," he said. "You get Jared up to Santa Fe all right yesterday?"

"Yes, in plenty of time to catch his flight." In her effort to avoid Ben, she had volunteered to drive their newest client to the airport. "He hadn't made any decision before he left, though."

And Tess still hadn't let up with her teasing. "I'm surprised he left at all," she said now. "But he told Caleb he'll be back soon. He seemed to like your personal attention."

Beside her, Ben shifted, giving her more room. She dropped her bag on the seat between them. Refusing to look his way, she said lightly, "Well, you know what we tell all our clients. 'You've come to the Wright Place.'"

Caleb chuckled. "Yeah, I heard that not too long ago."

"And it turned out to be true, didn't it?" Tess asked.

"Yep. That's why we're here celebrating tonight."

She elbowed him. "I'm not talking about the ranch."

He dropped a kiss on her temple.

Ben turned to Dana. "Kids home with Anne?"

His voice sounded stiff to her ears, but the other two didn't seem to notice. "No. She has a date tonight."

"With her high school hero," Tess said.

Dana grabbed a taco chip from the bowl on the table and nearly buried it in the salsa.

"The kids are at the Whistlestop with Nate," Tess went on. "She had a fit when she heard supper was adults-only."

We're adults, Ben had said the night Dana had almost let him kiss her. Again. *We can stop bickering all on our own.*

But they couldn't.

"Mom promised her a barbecue," Tess continued, "so

naturally, she wanted Lissa to come and stay the night. Mom and Aunt El are thrilled to have all the kids sleeping over, too. They were just complaining the other day about not sitting for them in so long."

Just as Ben had complained about not getting to see enough of the kids.

When Dori came to the booth, Dana ordered the first thing that came into her head. Tacos. A bad choice, reminding her of the day Ben had bought lunch for her family and Lissa's friends. Reminding her of all the days he'd spent at the house lately.

And bringing her thoughts to Monday night after the meeting. He'd gone from amorous to arrogant, in the space of a few heartbeats. All for the best, of course. His response had only made her more determined to keep her distance, before they did anything *else* they would both regret.

He seemed to remember the wisdom of that, too. When he'd dropped by the office the day before, he'd kept his visit all business and brief. Too brief for her liking.

Now, nothing seemed to satisfy her about their relationship. Maybe because the only thing she wanted was a *close* relationship. One everyone could know about. And she couldn't have that.

Sitting beside him, listening to his voice, hearing his laugh… Every minute felt like a punishment for a longing she had no way to control.

During supper, she struggled to keep her mind on the conversation. At the same time, she counted the minutes until they would finish eating and she could go home.

Late in the evening, she caught Tess eyeing her, making her sit up and—belatedly—pay attention. What had she missed? And why did Tess look so uncomfortable?

"Aunt El's spent a lot of time pounding the pavement this week," Tess said. "To prove there's support for the monument, she's getting names on a petition and plans to bring it to the next council meeting."

"Has she?" Ben asked. "Going to be an interesting night."

"Kayla and I aren't worried." Dana spoke with an assurance she didn't feel. The council members would vote for the playground. They had to.

If she needed to depend on Ben and his deciding vote, she might as well put their proposal through the office shredder. He would never support her, even if she tried to win him over to her opinion. Besides, how could she get close enough to talk to him at all, when he claimed he could read her so well?

If he could truly see into her heart, what he found would drive him away from her. Would push him toward voting against her.

What did it matter? They could never come to an agreement.

He wanted to honor his best friend. And she wanted no part of the memorial.

SUPPER FINISHED, THE FOUR of them strolled outside to the patio. Dana half listened as Ben told Tess and Caleb about a new mare he'd bought for the ranch. While they talked, she looked beyond the patio to a sky studded with stars.

A beautiful night, a night for lovers.

As if Caleb had heard Dana's thought, he pulled Tess close and said, "Since Nate's spoken for this evening, the two of us are going off for some alone time."

In the light of the tin lanterns on the patio tables, Tess blushed and looked at Dana, who swallowed her smile.

Caleb turned to Ben. "You don't mind taking Dana home?"   .

She caught her breath. Her earlier suspicions returned, and she shot another look at Tess. Did the color in her face really come from a blush, or had her cheeks flushed in guilty embarrassment? Had Tess known what Caleb was going to ask Ben? Had she put him up to it to begin with? Dana tried to push away the thought that Ben's invitation to supper had all been part of a plan. *Not Tess.*

Besides, as Dana had told Kayla, even Ellamae and Roselynn wouldn't have dreamed of matching her up with Ben.

"No problem," he said now. "I can drop Dana at the house."

And what could she say in return? She couldn't insist that the newlyweds drive her home. Feeling guilty for harboring even a fleeting suspicion of her own best friend, she simply nodded.

They walked out to the front of the café, where Tess had left their SUV and where Dana now noted Ben's truck parked up near the corner.

She wrapped her hands around her arms, chilled not from the October air but from the knowledge that she'd have to accept the ride home with Ben. After all the objections he had raised the night of the council meeting, she would never convince him to let her walk home alone.

Not at this hour.

Not even in the safest town in the state.

They said their farewells and walked away. Dana held her head high and kept her eyes focused on his truck. He claimed to be able to read her face. To see her feelings in her eyes. Though she wouldn't admit it then, even to herself, she acknowledged now that she knew exactly what he'd seen in her eyes on Monday night outside Town Hall.

The same thing he'd seen the night they'd stood so close together in her utility room.

Well, he wouldn't see it tonight. Not if she could help it. She continued to keep her eyes focused and her face forward and her tone light as they chatted all the way home.

All the way to the house Ben owned.

"Thanks for the ride," she said, her hand on the passenger door handle.

"I'll walk you in."

That's not necessary had been her battle cry for weeks now, and where had it gotten her? Nowhere with Ben. He never listened to anything.

Other than that, she had to admit, he excelled at everything, whether it involved ranching or handyman chores or caring for her kids. And as a perfect gentleman, since he'd driven her home—not just followed her—of course he would insist upon seeing her to the door.

To her surprise, as they went up the front path, he said, "Since we didn't stay for one of Dori's desserts, I thought you might pour me a cup of coffee." From inside the house, the dog yipped. "I haven't seen Duchess in a couple of days. And," he added, "I'd like to talk for a bit."

"Talk?"

"Yeah, talk. You know, conversation. Words back and forth. You and me."

More than likely, he wanted to discuss something to do with the house or the office. "I don't know. The last time we tried that, things didn't work out very well." She held back a sigh of exasperation at herself. Did they really need the reminder?

"If you keep the cookies coming, we ought to be fine."

Shaking her head, she said, "You're as bad as the kids." But Duchess had begun barking in earnest now. Dana led him inside.

While he greeted the dog, she went to the kitchen to fill the coffeemaker and the teakettle. Duchess padded into the room and bounded into her bed in the corner.

"The cookie jar's in the utility room," she told Ben. "Second shelf on the left. Beside the box of cereal."

To quote him, those directions "ought to be fine," too. They would have to, because she wasn't venturing anywhere near that room with him again. Her face warmed, reminding her of Tess's flush earlier. Now she couldn't tell if her own warmth came from a blush or guilty embarrassment. But she knew the trigger came from her memory of what had happened in that utility room a few short days ago.

Crossed signals.

She'd attempted to make that plain to him, too. She'd tried to explain about the mixed messages between them, though she knew in her heart she was to blame for most of them—bickering with him one moment and staring at him like a starstruck schoolgirl the next. Staring openly enough to give him the idea she'd wanted him to kiss her. Again.

Yet, that night in the utility room, all he had done was touch her wrist, and she had melted against him.

Well…all right, she hadn't quite let herself go to that extent.

But she'd wanted to.

For sure, she had trembled. For certain, he had felt it. No denying that. She could tell by the way he'd looked her up and down and then stared, his expression frozen.

She'd wanted him the night of Tess's wedding, too.

She would want him forever….

"You okay?"

Startled, she placed a couple of dessert plates on the table with a clatter. "Yes."

"You look out of it. Maybe you need a good night's sleep."

"Maybe."

"Lucky for you, all the kids went to stay at the Whistle-stop again." He lifted the lid of the cookie jar. "Chocolate chip, huh?"

She nodded, on the verge of nervous laughter. Obviously

good old Ben didn't feel *he'd* gotten lucky. Or maybe he felt he had—with the cookies. She ought to be glad to have such an…honorable friend. She ought to be doubly glad he hadn't mentioned that other night when quiet surrounded the two of them and no children slept upstairs.

"You wanted to talk?" she prompted, pouring her tea and his coffee.

"Yeah."

He took a cookie from the jar. "Chocolate chip are my favorite. Remember when you used to make them for me in your cooking class in eighth grade?"

She remembered. She'd thought of it the night of the wedding, too, when he'd asked her about "his" cookies. Was that why she'd baked these yesterday before taking Jared to the airport?

"Not just for you," she said. "Tess and I gave the burned cookies to all the guys."

He laughed.

Turning from the counter with their mugs, she saw he had taken P.J.'s place at the table, which put him closer to her than usual. But if she walked all the way around to Lissa's side to get some distance from him, they would sit facing one another.

She took her regular seat next to the baby's high chair. "I'm sure you didn't come in to discuss the cookie of the week, even if they are your favorite. What do we need to talk about, the house or the office?"

"The memorial."

She had lifted her brimming mug almost to her lips. Her hand jerked. Boiling water sloshed onto her fingers. She nearly dropped the mug onto the table, then grabbed her napkin and dabbed at her hand.

"Did you get burned?"

He reached for her, but she jerked her hand away, deliberately this time. "Don't worry about it. I told you, how I feel about the monument is my business."

"I heard that. I can see it. Tonight at supper, Caleb and Tess could, too. Didn't you notice how they reacted? Do you want everyone else seeing it, too?" His voice rose.

Duchess yelped. He waited until she had settled down again before continuing in a lower voice, "I have to tell you, folks are damned excited about that memorial, and even more excited about the fact they're dedicating it to a man they admire. How are they going to feel, every time they make mention of it, when that man's own wife looks like she can't stand to think about it?"

"I don't look—"

"You sure as hell do. And is that what you want them to see? Is that what you want your kids to notice every time their daddy's name is mentioned?" He stood abruptly, the chair legs screeching on the kitchen floor. "Come with me."

"What?"

But he had left the room.

Angry now, she followed through the doorway. He was already headed toward the stairs. "Where are you going?"

"I want to show you something in P.J.'s room."

"What does he have to do with this?" she asked.

But he didn't answer.

Upstairs, he went into her son's room.

Following close on his heels, she came to a halt just inside the doorway.

Everything looked the same as usual, from the dinosaur-patterned quilt she had made for P.J.'s bed, to the row of baseball caps hanging from pegs on the closet door, to the plastic jar on one end of his dresser. The jar of washers he'd carried with him almost everywhere since Ben had given it to him.

Ben had replaced the overhead light fixture a couple of

weeks ago, but other than that, she could find nothing different. "What is it I'm supposed to see?"

"This." He reached up between the dresser and the doorway and tapped a picture frame hanging on the wall.

Paul's photograph.

She took a half step backward, but he caught her hand and drew her into the room. Then he took her by the shoulders and turned her to face the photo, the original of the small picture P.J. had left on the coffee table downstairs.

"And this." He tapped the row of medals on the uniform. "Paul earned every one of these for skill and bravery and honor. For fighting to help people who couldn't help themselves. For saving lives. And if that's not enough for you, just think about what else he did. He gave *his* life for his country."

She heard him inhale and exhale slowly. Felt his breath ruffle her hair and his hands lift from her shoulders.

"That makes him a hero," he said, his voice hard now. "A hero in anyone's eyes—but yours."

His boot heels struck the wooden floor when he backed away from her, as if he couldn't stand to be near her. In the dresser mirror, she saw his reflection. His face looked pinched, his eyes sad. "You married that man and had children with him, but even for their sake, you can't honor him the way he deserves. You loved him, but—"

"I *didn't* love him."

"What?"

She looked at his reflection again and wanted to cry at the look on his face. At the truth of how she felt about him. At the memory of his reaction when he'd realized her feelings. And most of all, at the lies he and everyone else in her life believed about Paul.

The lies she had fed them.

She turned to face him. "I didn't love him," she said. "I did when I married him, but not...at the end."

He shook his head as if stunned. "He loved you."

"No, he didn't. Paul loved—" she flung her arm out and pointed at the photograph on the wall "—*that*. Being a hero. Being a football star. Being looked up to and admired and—and *honored*. Paul loved the image of Paul."

"You're wrong. He was my best friend, and I knew him as well as anyone could. Better than you did, obviously."

"You didn't know him at all." The words had tumbled out before she could stop them. He looked as if she'd slapped him. "He liked you, yes. But for the most part, he liked what you could do for him."

"No—"

"Yes. Think back. Who drilled history and geography into him when he didn't study for exams in grade school? Who covered for him with the principal when he got in trouble in junior high? Who always picked up the checks when we went to the Double S after the high school football games?" Her voice cracked, and she swallowed hard. "Who drove me home from parties when he couldn't stand to leave the crowd?"

"He was my friend. I didn't mind doing any of those things for him."

"You didn't have a choice. He may never have fumbled a ball in his life, but he'd have dropped you in a minute if you'd stopped providing what he wanted. I'm sorry, Ben, but he used you. The way he used me and anyone else he could."

"I don't buy a word of that. And how can you say those things about him? He was a damned good husband—"

"He wasn't."

That stopped him, but not for long. "All right, maybe not in your eyes. But he was a good provider and a good daddy—"

"He wasn't either of those."

"Oh, come on." He grimaced and shook his head. "Next thing, you'll be telling me he never existed."

"He existed, all right," she said. "He just hid the real Paul behind the image he let everyone see."

"Dammit, I don't believe this." He brushed past her. "And I'm not staying around to listen to it."

His boots thudded against the stairs.

She curled her fingers into fists, then winced as the skin pulled taut on her scalded hand. Her eyes blurred with tears. Not from the pain of her blistered fingers but from the irony of their heated words. She'd done such a good job of lying, Ben couldn't believe her when she told the truth.

Downstairs, the front door slammed.

The sound of it echoed through the quiet house, reminding her she would be alone all night.

Except for the dog.

Chapter Sixteen

Halfway home again, Ben made a last-minute decision at a crossroads, swinging the truck onto a side road that would take him even farther out of town. His thoughts had swung twice as fast—several times over—since he'd barreled out of Dana's house.

Instead of leaving her at the door, as he probably should have, he'd gone inside. He'd wanted answers to all the things troubling him. Instead, he'd left there a hell of a lot more troubled, with way too many questions—old and new—in his mind.

Questions he had no plans to share with anyone.

This time on a Friday evening, he'd have found no one at the ranch to listen to him anyway. His foreman and all his ranch hands would have gone their own ways, maybe into town for the high school varsity game or out on the back highway to one of the bars for a brew. Neither of those choices attracted him tonight. He didn't want to be on his own—didn't want to give all those questions in his head free rein. Still, he disliked the idea of facing a crowd. Strange, since he usually liked being out with folks.

He and Paul both had.

A few miles later, he pulled up to a ranch house much like his own, knowing he'd have a good chance of finding a family man like Sam Robertson at home. Sure enough,

Sam answered the door with his five-year-old peeking out from behind him.

"Hey, Ben, have a seat. Be right back. Becky and I were just going into the kitchen to see her mama." He turned to his daughter and signed the words as he said aloud, "Ready for your bedtime snack?"

Looking at Ben, she grinned and tapped the fingertips of one hand against her other palm.

"I know that one," he said, copying her motion. "Cookies, right?" He tried not to think about…the chocolate chips he'd just left behind.

Sam nodded. "Yep. Want a beer? Coffee? Sweet tea?"

"Tea sounds good." He didn't want to think about the coffee he'd missed out on, either. He took a seat on one of the living room couches and looked at the chime clock on the mantel. Earlier than he'd figured. The conversation he'd planned to have with Dana hadn't gone nearly as long as he'd expected.

Sam came back into the room carrying two tall glasses.

Ben took a swig and looked at Sam, who had settled back on the other couch. The two of them had been friends for a long time—as long as he'd known Paul. If anyone could swap memories with him, Sam could. If anyone would tell him the truth, Sam would.

And he wanted some truths.

Not about Dana. Those, he'd have to hear from her own lips, if she'd ever share them.

He swallowed another mouthful of tea. "I left the post digger out by the barn."

"Good timing. Caleb wants it for next week."

The two of them talked for a while, and eventually, as Ben had known it would, the conversation came around to Paul.

"Kayla told me about the monument," Sam said. "A good idea."

"Yeah." Too bad everyone didn't think so. He frowned, recalling what Dana had said about her life with Paul. What he had no intention of believing. "I'm glad folks came up with the proposal and followed through on presenting it to the council."

"Paul would have been, too."

"You mean that folks want to honor him?"

"And to look up to him like we always did."

The statement came too close to Dana's accusations for comfort. "We can't blame him for that."

"Of course not. He was used to having us all hanging around the biggest fish we'd ever had in our little pond. You'd know that more than the rest of us."

"Yeah." Just what did he know? Nothing, according to Dana. "Did you ever think he took all that attention for granted?" That was as close as he would go to asking a question he didn't really need an answer to. It was crazy for him to wonder about it. To let Dana's distorted thoughts affect his own.

But Sam laughed. "Ben, I think he took everything he could get and wanted more. And I'll tell you another thing. When they set up that monument, they'd better make sure it's something fancy, something big and hard to miss—just like him. That's what he'd have wanted, too."

Ben's memories rang true. He had to respect them.

Much as he hated to admit it, he had to allow Dana the right to her feelings, too.

But he had memories and feelings of his own, and they were all tied up with what that monument meant to him.

A physical representation of the honor Paul deserved. An honor he—as Paul's closest friend—would make every effort to uphold.

A permanent reminder that he had to do his best for Dana and her young family, though she fought him every step of the way.

A mocking remembrance that he'd waited too long to tell her the truth about his promise.

And a deathblow to any chance he might have with her.

DANA PADDED BAREFOOT into the bathroom. Her feet stung from the cold tiles. Her eyes stung, too. As she switched on the light and opened the medicine chest, she avoided looking at her reflection. She'd already caught sight of her face in her bedroom mirror, and it wasn't pretty. Not surprising, after the night she'd put herself through.

Or half a night. When she'd rolled out of bed just now, her alarm clock had read 3:37 a.m.

Her face looked puffy. Her hair sprouted in different directions. Her blistered hand throbbed.

And she'd left the ointment in the living room.

Groaning, she went down the hall, headed toward the stairs. Halfway along, she stopped. After a long battle with herself, she went into P.J.'s room and turned on the lamp on his nightstand. Then she sat on the edge of his bed, took a deep breath and brushed her hand across a dinosaur on his quilt.

She didn't want to look at the other side of the room.

In any other photo she'd ever seen of Paul, he'd had his mouth curved in a confident grin and his chin held high, tilting his head into his favorite look-at-me-and-love-me angle.

And she had loved him. All through school, he was the boy of her dreams, and after graduation she had married him. Yet, a few years later she'd felt only relief when they'd agreed that their marriage was over.

When it came to being a husband and father, he'd left a

lot to be desired. Then he had gone overseas with his platoon, where he'd earned all those medals he wore.

In everyone's eyes but hers, he'd gone from strength to strength, from golden boy to brave soldier to war hero. In the meantime, she'd kept up appearances, and when he came home on leave, she'd made that one last-ditch effort to save their marriage. Only days later, he was killed.

For the folks in Flagman's Folly, and especially for her children's sake, she could never do anything to destroy Paul's image.

Not when she'd spent so many years helping to preserve it.

She couldn't risk getting close to Ben, no matter how much she wanted to. As it was, she'd told him too much tonight.

At last she looked across the room at the photograph on the wall. Paul stared back at her with the most serious expression she'd ever seen on him in a photo. Or, come to think of it, in real life.

Sighing, she rose from the bed.

The doorbell rang. She gasped, then hurried to the stairs, her thoughts flying to her children. To the fear any mother would have when a bell pealed in the middle of the night and her child wasn't home.

To the sight of Tess standing on the front porch, waiting to tell her—

She flung the door wide.

Not Tess.

Ben.

"I thought—" she blurted. "The kids?"

"No," he said quickly. "No, nothing about the kids."

Exhaling in relief, she sagged against the door.

Duchess had run into the room and wove in and out between them. Only half aware of doing so, Dana stooped to pat the puppy. Duchess wriggled in excitement, accepted a head-scratching from Ben and then padded back to the kitchen.

Dana stood and looked at Ben, her eyebrows raised.

"I…saw your light on," he said.

"Oh." She blinked. "And you thought you'd…drop in."

"Well, I never did get my coffee."

She stared at him in disbelief. He wanted more than coffee. He wanted to pick up their conversation again. At this hour.

That was Ben, though. She knew him well.

He'd never give up on anything. Never break a promise. Never leave a friend hanging. Never want to let the sun go down—or in this case, come up—on an argument. It had both surprised and startled her when he'd slammed out of there last night.

Now they might as well get this over with.

Once and for all.

She stepped back. When he moved past her, she closed the door. "Have you been sitting outside the house all night?"

"No. I headed home and then…drove around for a while."

"Have a seat. I'll bring the coffee out here. Give me a few minutes."

Or a few hours.

At one point in her presentation, she stopped, realizing she was going through the same motions she had on the night they'd made love. Now, she shivered. Not in excitement or anticipation but in fear. Because she wanted Ben's arms around her again. *No matter what.*

Then she thought of her kids. Of Clarice and the rest of the townsfolk. Of seeing how only a portion of the truth had hurt Ben.

Compared to all that, what she wanted couldn't even make the list.

It wasn't until she brewed the coffee and returned to the living room and saw the way he looked at her that she realized she'd run downstairs in her sleepwear.

Oh, well. Serve him right for all the times he'd walked around here shirtless.

Too bad he'd get less of a thrill than she ever had eyeing him. Lissa had passed the nightshirt on to her, labeling it "babyish." It covered more of her than the gown she had worn for Tess's wedding…the gown Ben had unbuttoned later that night.

In any case, the picture of the smiling teapot on the nightshirt went perfectly with the plate she carried.

"Here," she said, holding it out to him. "You never got your chocolate chip cookies, either."

DANA HAD SAID SHE DIDN'T WANT any of the cookies, so he polished them off. Once in a while, he sipped from his mug. She had taken a seat on the other end of the couch, and they sat there in silence. After all, he told her he'd come for the coffee. Why would she sit there and chat?

Why would he start a conversation?

Because he *had* to. Just as he'd had to come here again.

After talking to Sam, after spending hours driving the back roads in his pickup truck, he'd finally admitted he couldn't stay away. He had to know everything Dana had kept from him.

From the corner of his eye he took in her bare calf, the curve of her knee and the swell of her breasts beneath the soft nightgown.

Leaning forward, he set his empty plate onto the table. At the sight of the scrunched-up tube of ointment, he frowned, remembering. She had burned her hand in the kitchen earlier.

Looking over at the plate, she said, "I assume you want to talk again."

He waited until she turned his way. "That, too. But I also want to listen." Her eyes widened, revealing how much his words had surprised her. He waited, giving her time to get her expression under control again. Then he said, "Tell me about Paul."

"What do you want to know?"

Her shoulders went back, and he knew he'd better take it slowly. Better start with details less upsetting to her. He settled against the couch and rested his coffee mug on his thigh. "Tell me about the scholarship."

She frowned. "He didn't get one."

"That's what I meant."

She shifted, putting more space between them. Deliberately or not, he didn't know.

"He'd pinned his hopes on winning a scholarship somewhere. When he got passed over in the draft by his first choice and then his second choice and finally all his other choices, he decided to go to State." She looked down at her hands in her lap. "Even there, when he made the team, he couldn't get his star quarterback status again."

She'd lowered her voice, as if trying to soften her words. To ease his disappointment. To help him deal with the truth.

"Because he *wasn't* a star," she continued. "Here in Flagman's Folly, yes, where everyone had his back and made him look good. But not at State. There, he wasn't even a team player. They'd cut him before the third game."

He tightened his fingers around the coffee mug. "That's when he came home?"

"Yes."

"You said…" *He wasn't a good husband.*

Hell, he couldn't ask her about that, though he wanted to know. What happened between husband and wife had to stay there. But she'd told him something else, too. "You said he wasn't a good provider."

"No." She smoothed the afghan resting on the arm of the couch. "You know after he came back, he took the job at the dealership. Mostly because he liked the idea of being the superstar car salesman. And he did make some sales over the years. But with the economy so bad, he didn't make many."

He clenched his free hand into a fist. "Geez, Dana. He could've borrowed from me—"

"No, he couldn't. Because then people would know. They'd see the real Paul behind the image."

"I wouldn't have told anyone."

"No, you wouldn't." She sounded sad. "You'd have covered for him. The way you always did. And he knew that."

"Then why didn't he come to me?"

"Because I told him if he asked you for money, I would spread the news to everyone in Flagman's Folly."

"You—" He choked on the word. *"Why?"*

"Because he would have been using you, the way he'd always done. And I couldn't stand to see it happen again." Her fingers dug into the afghan. "Ben, he gambled away the commissions he made from the dealership."

He shook his head. "I would've known—"

"No, you couldn't have. He didn't do it here, just for that reason. *Folks would know.* He lost most of it in out-of-town casinos, and the rest he spent buying things online. Status symbols, to show off his wealth—what little he had left."

The longer she talked the faster the words came. He didn't want to hear any more. But he had to listen.

"When that ran out, he turned to me. The economy hadn't done much for real estate, either. Still, he took every penny he could get—every penny I could squeeze from my business without going under." She exhaled a shaky breath and met his eyes. Hers were filled with a pain he had no trouble reading. "He took food from the kids' mouths. But he didn't care, because no one would know."

"Damn," he muttered. "*I* didn't know. I—"

"Don't," she said. "It's the image he wanted you to see. We all have those. Just as we have things we want to hide."

Her words cut him with their toneless accusation, a reminder of the secret he'd kept from her. Of the promise he'd made.

He set his mug on the coffee table and rose from the couch. He had come back here again looking for answers. But he'd never expected to hear all this.

It mocked everything he had known about Paul. Everything he'd done for him.

Everything he hadn't done for himself.

All this time, he had stayed away from Dana, believing he couldn't touch her. Believing he owed Paul that loyalty.

Now, getting hit with all this…

He shook his head. "I can't believe it. The man died a hero, Dana."

Eyes gleaming, she looked away.

Chapter Seventeen

Dana spent the weekend with the kids...and without Ben. Fortunately they had the puppy to keep them all occupied. Yet even Duchess couldn't hold P.J.'s attention full-time.

On Sunday afternoon, as she sat on the couch folding clothes, he'd climbed up to sit beside her.

"Where's Ben, Mama?" he asked. "He doesn't like us anymore?"

She'd expected something like that. Hadn't she known having Ben around the house so often wasn't the best thing for the kids? She had to swallow hard before she could respond. "I'm sure he's busy working on his ranch today."

"I miss him."

"I know you do," she'd said. *So do I.*

On Monday, with things so quiet, she suggested Tess take the day off for more honeymoon time, to run errands, for whatever she liked. And when Tess took her up on the offer, she sagged in guilty relief.

She welcomed the chance to spend the time alone in the office. But by late afternoon, the quiet had gotten to her. The walls had begun to close in. She'd had too much time to think.

She left work early for a quick trip to Harley's on her way home. And even there, standing at the head of the pet-products aisle, she found her thoughts straying to Ben.

He'd looked shell-shocked by everything she had said. It destroyed her to know how much she'd hurt him. But she couldn't keep the truth hidden any longer. Not from him.

That second time, he had left the house quietly. No slamming the door behind him. No puppy bounding in from the kitchen to investigate. That time, she had felt so much worse. Because his careful closing of the door made his departure final.

Yet it also made it more like Ben. That was his way. Not to make waves, not to cause trouble, just to be there, steady, reliable, safe. Always.

Though not for her, from now on.

"Excuse me," an unmistakable—and unmistakably teasing—voice said from behind her. Tess pushed her cart beside Dana's. Eyebrows raised, she pointed toward the aisle. "Don't you need to go down there?"

Tess's question didn't surprise her. "I hate to tell you this," Dana said, "but your expression of wide-eyed innocence stopped working in the third grade. And no, I don't need dog food. The puppy came with a good supply. As you probably knew before I did."

"Okay, I confess. You never mentioned her at the Double S the other night, but Mom and Aunt El did happen to *share the news.*"

"Of course." Dana forced herself to laugh along with Tess.

"That's just like Ben."

She winced. "Mmm-hmm." Hoping Tess hadn't seen her reaction or the sudden moisture in her eyes, she hurried to push her cart toward the checkout counter. "Hi, Billy."

The clerk looked from her to Tess and back again. "What are you doing here? I saw Anne on her way to pick up P.J. and Stacey. She said you had the council meeting today."

"Later tonight," she said. After she'd paid for her groceries, she stepped aside to wait for Tess.

She wanted to run out of the store immediately. To pass on attending the meeting altogether. To avoid seeing Ben. But of course she couldn't let Kayla down. Besides, where would she go? Everyone in Flagman's Folly knew she should be at Town Hall tonight. And unless she invented an excuse, she couldn't even hide out at home. She'd arranged for Anne to stay with the kids.

"Ready?" Tess asked her.

"Ready as I'll ever be," she said grimly.

Tess frowned, and Dana pushed her cart through the automatic doors. In the parking lot, they stopped behind Tess's SUV.

"Anyway," Tess said as she unloaded her groceries from the cart, "back to what I was saying inside. That was nice of Ben to take care of the dog food. *And* to get the puppy for the kids."

"Yes. He's a good friend."

"Is he? A *friend,* I mean?"

"Of course," she snapped. "We might have different opinions over things, but that doesn't mean we can't be friends."

"Hey, girl."

Dana blushed. "Sorry. I was thinking about something else."

"I have a feeling it's all related." Tess leaned back against the SUV. "I won't give you the wide-eyed innocent look again. But around the time that stopped working for you, I think we discovered boys. Dana," she added softly, "you know what I meant by the emphasis on that word just now. It's obvious Ben wants to be more than a friend."

"He can't be."

"Why not?"

She looked around the lot, empty of other shoppers at that moment. Empty of a possible distraction. Trapped, she looked back at Tess again. "You know why. And he's only being nice because of Paul."

Tess shook her head. "Oh, no, he's not."

"We're just friends," Dana insisted. "Besides, if I... If we..." She gripped the handle of the shopping cart. "I could never live it down."

"Live what down?"

She groaned. "You're going to make me say it, aren't you? All right, then. Folks would never forgive Paul's wife and Paul's best friend for crossing that line."

"That's not true."

"Yes, it is." She sighed. "You should hear Clarice rant about it. She's appalled that Ben is at the house so often—and there's not even anything going on between us."

Not anymore.

"Clarice is a wonderful woman," Tess said, "but she's never gotten over losing Vernon. She's let his death affect too many things in her life. Don't let her get to you, Dana. Clarice is *not* the voice of Flagman's Folly."

Dana's guilt eased just the smallest bit. "All right, maybe not, but Ellamae is."

Tess laughed, and despite her mixed emotions—or maybe because of them—Dana couldn't keep from smiling, too.

"You're right," Tess said. "Or at least, Aunt El thinks she is. But she doesn't feel the way Clarice does. She and Mom think you and Ben make a perfect couple."

That statement made her reel. "No—"

"*Yes.* You know I wouldn't lie to you. Everyone in town thinks that."

"I don't believe it," she blurted, then shivered at her accidental echo of Ben's words. "No one has ever said anything like this to me before. Why not? And why are you saying it now?"

"Because they were giving you time. Letting you grieve. But I'm *your* best friend, and I'm saying it now because it *is* time."

"You mean, you think that, too?"

Tess nodded. "I'll confess, I have for years. I don't want to hurt you," she added, her voice soft again, "but I saw how things were with you and Paul. You've been ready for a while. You need to move on. You *and* Ben."

Dana stared across the empty parking lot. Everything Tess had said stunned her. Her final admission took her breath away.

She had a confession of her own to tell, but she couldn't share it with Tess now. She couldn't admit Ben had already moved on.

And the quiet closing of the door behind him said he wouldn't be back again.

DANA SAT IN THE FRONT ROW of spectators' seats in the courtroom and braced herself as Ben announced the next items on the agenda. The proposals.

Whispers broke out all around her, then quieted, until she heard nothing in the room but the blades of the overhead fan. Obviously the time had come to address the topic of most interest to folks this evening.

Which proposal had received Ben's all-important vote? Had he supported the playground? Or had he voted the way he had planned all along—to choose the memorial and stay loyal to his best friend?

No sense worrying about it, when she already knew what decision he had made.

She should have known from the beginning, from the night of Tess's wedding, when he'd told her about the promise he'd made. Now, weeks later, that news still made her breath catch. No matter what he claimed about being friends, for all these months since Paul's death, he'd thought of her as less than that. He'd considered her his *responsibility.* That knowledge hurt more than she could ever have imagined.

Just as she had hurt him with the truth about Paul.

They couldn't be...close. She'd made sure they couldn't be friends. And now he had decided against her proposal.

How could she expect anything else?

Still, holding on to hope, she had tried to talk to him since her arrival tonight. But like the previous meeting when she had refused to make eye contact, he now avoided her.

At the front table, he cleared his throat and moved his water glass aside. Nervous gestures that astounded her. In all the years she had known him, Ben Sawyer had never once felt nervous about speaking in public.

He couldn't face her because he'd decided against her proposal.

And she was going to live for the rest of her life with a permanent, public reminder of all the mistakes she had made.

"Folks," he began, "as you know, the council was recently presented with two proposals, both involving property adjacent to the elementary school." Reading from the paper in front of him, he said, "The first proposal recommends that a memorial be erected on that site to honor Paul Wright, one of our own local heroes. A man who gave his life for his country."

No one made a sound. Dana locked her fingers in her lap.

"The second proposal," he continued, "recommends the building of a playground on that same site, to provide a common area for the children of Flagman's Folly." He set the papers aside and looked up at his audience. "The council considered both proposals very carefully and came to—" he paused "—an impasse."

The whispers broke out again. He waited until they had trailed away. "As a result," he said slowly, "the council has an alternative suggestion to present to both committees."

She exchanged a glance with Kayla.

Then she looked across the aisle at Tess, who gave a tiny shrug. Beside her, Ellamae wore a disgruntled expression. Obviously neither her gossip-gathering skill nor the power of Judge Baylor had helped her this time.

Dana faced forward again. Ben sat looking directly at her. She jumped. Hoping he hadn't noticed, she pressed her fingers more tightly together.

He had always claimed he could read her face. She wished she could read his. But she couldn't—because there was nothing to see. No expression. No emotion. No feelings for her at all.

He looked away.

"The council," he continued, "recommends the committees meet on a middle ground. We would like to support the intent to honor Paul Wright with a memorial—" his gaze met Dana's again briefly, then moved out to survey the room "—by suggesting the two committees merge, name the playground after the Wright family, and dedicate it to Paul and Dana's children and all the children of Flagman's Folly."

A hush fell over the courtroom, as if everyone in it had taken a deep breath.

A similar quiet had filled the cemetery the day they'd laid Paul to rest. Dana did now what she couldn't do then.

Fight back tears.

AFTER SENDING ANNE HOME with Billy, Dana went to kiss all three of her sleeping kids. She patted Duchess, curled up in the bed that had somehow made its way upstairs to the floor in P.J.'s room. One corner of the dinosaur quilt trailed down beside the puppy, as if P.J. had tried to tuck her in for the night.

Downstairs in the living room again, she curled up on the couch, tucking herself in with the afghan. She tried not to think about the last time she had sat there with Ben.

The reaction to his announcement in the courtroom tonight left no doubt about how everyone in the room felt. After a quick conference with both committees, Ellamae immediately presented a revised proposal, which the council had unanimously passed.

Dana had left Town Hall as soon as she could.

She and Ben hadn't spoken a word to each other.

She pulled the afghan more closely around her. Through the long window beside the front door, she saw a truck glide past the house. The streetlamp gave off enough light to tell her the truck was Ben's.

Of course. He was on his way home.

Headlights flashed in the east window. He had turned into her driveway. She exhaled in a rush. Before he reached the steps, she had moved to the entryway and opened the door.

The cold night air made her shiver. Made her voice shake when she said, "I didn't want the bell to wake the kids."

Ben entered and closed the door firmly behind him.

When he said nothing, she asked, "You're just here to listen again?"

"At first, anyhow."

She nodded and led him into the living room.

He took a seat beside her on the couch.

She hadn't planned what she would tell him, if she ever got the chance to talk to him again. After tonight's meeting, she hadn't really expected to have the opportunity at all. But now that he had arrived, she felt no qualms.

This was Ben.

She took a deep breath. "I'll start. But first, there's something I need to know. You told me you had the deciding vote on the council."

He nodded.

"But there was a stalemate. That means you *didn't* vote."

"That's right."

"The committee's recommendation tonight—the compromise—that was your idea, wasn't it?"

"Yes. I knew how you felt about the memorial, but not why. Not in the beginning." He shook his head. "If I had, I might not have pushed as hard as I did for you to tell me your reasons. But even once I knew, when it came down to it, I still wanted to see Paul honored. Now he is, and his name will live on the way it should. Through his family."

She nodded. That was Ben, too. Of course, he would stand up for what he believed in. Would stay loyal and true.

"You're right," she said softly. "He was your best friend, in the only way he knew how to be. You need to honor that."

"You're okay with it?"

"I'm okay with it." She had managed to hold back earlier, but now she couldn't stop a tear from running down her cheek. She wiped it away. "After I left Town Hall, I stopped by the cemetery to make my peace with Paul. Thanks to you."

"Me?"

She nodded. "At the end of his life, he was a hero. You were right about that, too, all along. And it's what I want the kids to remember about him."

"The good parts." He smiled sadly. "The rest of what you told me, they don't need to know. No one does."

"No. But I want you to know *all* the parts."

"There's more?"

"There's more." Not that long ago she wouldn't have been able to share this with anyone. "You know how upset I get at the thought of you wanting to take care of me."

"That would be an understatement."

"Paul…" She hesitated. Maybe she still had more qualms than she'd thought. Not about trusting Ben, but about having to show him how naive she'd been. "I told you he used me, too. He built his ego by tearing mine down. He started early, long before high school, and never let up. It was so subtle back then, I didn't realize it."

Ben's eyes glimmered.

She swallowed hard. "When he came back from State, he wasn't subtle anymore, just told me outright I needed him and would never get anywhere without him. And I…I bought into it." Her laugh sounded bitter. "I was that dumb. But I'd never been with anyone else, and we'd been together since grade school. When he came home on leave that last time, I thought maybe things had changed for the better. He seemed different, as though he cared."

"He *was* different," Ben said in a low voice. "He did care. I told you, that's when he asked me to watch over you and the kids."

She nodded. "I believe now he meant well. But what he wanted for me isn't what I want." She spoke as quietly as he had. "I want to be a good mother to my kids. I don't ever want to be weak and needy—the way Paul claimed I was."

"*Dana.* You've been running a business and raising three children on your own for years. There's nothing weak about you. You're the strongest woman I know."

Her heart soared. She'd been so wrong, for so long, about so many things. But not this. Of course, Ben was nothing like Paul. Of course Ben believed in her.

"After he left again," she said, "I finally came to my

senses. I realized that, no matter what he said, I'd never been the kind of woman he claimed I was. And he'd long ago stopped being the man I'd once cared about. The man whose image I'd always tried so hard to protect." She took a deep breath and released it. "When he died, I felt I had to keep up that image. For the folks in town. For the kids. And especially for you. Because you were his best friend. And because…I love you."

Her voice broke, but she rushed on. "I know I shouldn't tell you, because we're just friends. But I can't help thinking that if I had said it months ago, we could have had a chance together. I could have had what I'd always wanted. A good daddy for my kids. A strong marriage. An equal partner."

"That's what I wanted," he said.

Wanted, not *want.*

Now her heart broke, too. She looked away.

"Dana." He took her hand. "A long time ago I made a big mistake by stepping back from what I wanted. Instead, I did what I could—for you and Paul—knowing you deserved the better man. Only now I know I'm the *best* man for you."

Slowly she turned to look at him.

He twined their fingers together. "Everything I stepped back from is what you've always wanted, too. The kids. The marriage. The equal partner. I wouldn't settle for anything less." Smiling, he added, "Since kindergarten, I wouldn't settle for anyone but you. I never changed my mind about that, and I never will."

He reached up with his free hand to brush away the tear running down her cheek. "I won't change my thoughts about taking care of you, either. I want us to take care of each other. Not because we're weak, but because that's what makes a marriage strong. That's what makes us equal partners. Can you see that?"

Not trusting herself to speak, she simply nodded.

"And I came up with that suggestion for the committees because I wanted you to understand a compromise would work. That you and I could reach our own middle ground." He tightened his fingers around hers and raised their joined hands. "We made it."

She laughed shakily. "Are you expecting me to argue with that?"

He shook his head. "No, just to love me. The way I've always loved you."

He wrapped his free arm around her and touched his lips to hers. His kiss was hot enough to satisfy the desire she'd fought for so long. Sweet enough to tell her he would *always* be the best man for her.

And filled with the kind of promise she'd want to hold him to forever.

Epilogue

One month later

On a cool, crisp Saturday morning, a week after their wedding, Ben stood on the playground holding Dana's hand. It was a nice day for the dedication.

Across from them, on a bench near the basketball court, Lissa sat watching them. When she caught him looking at her, she grinned and waved. Smiling, he waved back.

P.J. had joined a group of boys his own age playing kickball in the schoolyard.

Ben gently pushed the baby swing. Stacey gurgled, and he laughed.

"She's happy the committee let her christen the swingset," Dana said.

"Looks like it," he agreed. He caught his new wife's gaze. Just a short while ago, Ellamae had asked her to cut the ribbon for the dedication ceremony. "You're okay with your new job?"

"I'm glad for it," she said. "It will let me cut the ties to the past. The bad ties. And," she added in a softer tone, "it's a way for me to honor Paul."

His throat suddenly tight, he nodded.

Ellamae hurried up to them again. "Now, Dana, I hope you don't mind that Kayla's giving the dedication."

"Not at all. She did so much to make sure everything was ready for today, especially with all the additions."

He and Caleb and Sam had taken the initial proposal beyond just the play area for the kids. They would soon break ground for the new Flagman's Folly Community Center, too.

"I think Kayla deserves the pleasure," Dana added.

Ellamae looked at them both thoughtfully, then said, "They asked me to speak, but I recommended her." She laughed. "Between Becky and the new baby on the way, she'll have more to do with this playground than I will. Besides, I've taken care of enough around here already."

"You mean by joining the monument committee?" Dana asked.

"No. I mean, by *creating* the monument committee." She shook her head. "If I hadn't helped you two work through all those problems Paul caused between you, you never would've made a couple."

Dana's eyes widened in astonishment. "You knew about Paul?"

She nodded. "The way the Wrights spoiled their only son, there was no surprise he turned out the way he did," she said gruffly. "Besides, we'd had more than a few creditors calling Judge Baylor." She shrugged. "But all that's between us and the judge. And Stacey." She smiled at the baby.

Ben squeezed Dana's hand. "The important thing is," he said, "folks have always thought Dana and I should be together."

"Well, of course they have. Except Clarice. But don't worry, I'm working on her, and she's coming along." She gave an exaggerated sigh. "As usual, I'm the only one willing to do anything around here." She winked at them, then sauntered away.

He and Dana exchanged a glance.

He shook his head. "Think of all the time we wasted, and for nothing," he said.

"Think of all the time you waited," she countered, "and never stopped being my friend. Ben, there are so many things that haven't lasted for me. You will."

"Yep. Like nature taking its course." When she laughed, he wrapped his arms around her.

He'd never felt more content.

Just like the storybooks...

They would live happily ever after in the Land of Enchantment—otherwise known as the state of New Mexico.

Because Benjamin Franklin Sawyer had finally gotten his girl.

* * * * *

COMING NEXT MONTH from Harlequin®
American Romance®
AVAILABLE SEPTEMBER 4, 2012

#1417 DUKE: DEPUTY COWBOY
Harts of the Rodeo
Roz Denny Fox
Duke Adams is a solid, dependable lawman, great with kids and a champion bull rider. He'd be perfect—except Angie Barrington can't stand rodeo cowboys....

#1418 THE COWBOY SOLDIER'S SONS
Callahan Cowboys
Tina Leonard
Retired from military service, Shaman Phillips comes to Tempest, New Mexico, to find peace. The last thing he expects to find is a blonde bombshell who just might be the key to his redemption.

#1419 RESCUED BY A RANGER
Hill Country Heroes
Tanya Michaels
Hiding out in the Texas Hill Country, single mother Alex Hunt is living a lie. But can she keep her secrets from the irresistible lawman next door?

#1420 THE M.D.'S SECRET DAUGHTER
Safe Harbor Medical
Jacqueline Diamond
Eight years ago, after Dr. Zack Sargent betrayed her trust, Jan Garcia broke their engagement and moved away...never telling him she kept the child she was supposed to give up for adoption.

REQUEST YOUR FREE BOOKS!
2 FREE NOVELS PLUS 2 FREE GIFTS!

❧ Harlequin®

American ★ Romance®

LOVE, HOME & HAPPINESS

YES! Please send me 2 FREE Harlequin® American Romance® novels and my 2 FREE gifts (gifts are worth about $10). After receiving them, if I don't wish to receive any more books, I can return the shipping statement marked "cancel." If I don't cancel, I will receive 4 brand-new novels every month and be billed just $4.49 per book in the U.S. or $5.24 per book in Canada. That's a saving of at least 14% off the cover price! It's quite a bargain! Shipping and handling is just 50¢ per book in the U.S. and 75¢ per book in Canada.* I understand that accepting the 2 free books and gifts places me under no obligation to buy anything. I can always return a shipment and cancel at any time. Even if I never buy another book, the two free books and gifts are mine to keep forever.

154/354 HDN FEP2

Name	(PLEASE PRINT)

Address	Apt. #

City	State/Prov.	Zip/Postal Code

Signature (if under 18, a parent or guardian must sign)

Mail to the **Reader Service**:
IN U.S.A.: P.O. Box 1867, Buffalo, NY 14240-1867
IN CANADA: P.O. Box 609, Fort Erie, Ontario L2A 5X3

Not valid for current subscribers to Harlequin American Romance books.

Want to try two free books from another line?
Call 1-800-873-8635 or visit www.ReaderService.com.

* Terms and prices subject to change without notice. Prices do not include applicable taxes. Sales tax applicable in N.Y. Canadian residents will be charged applicable taxes. Offer not valid in Quebec. This offer is limited to one order per household. All orders subject to credit approval. Credit or debit balances in a customer's account(s) may be offset by any other outstanding balance owed by or to the customer. Please allow 4 to 6 weeks for delivery. Offer available while quantities last.

Your Privacy—The Reader Service is committed to protecting your privacy. Our Privacy Policy is available online at www.ReaderService.com or upon request from the Reader Service.

We make a portion of our mailing list available to reputable third parties that offer products we believe may interest you. If you prefer that we not exchange your name with third parties, or if you wish to clarify or modify your communication preferences, please visit us at www.ReaderService.com/consumerschoice or write to us at Reader Service Preference Service, P.O. Box 9062, Buffalo, NY 14269. Include your complete name and address.

Welcome to the Texas Hill Country! In the third book in Tanya Michaels's series HILL COUNTRY HEROES, *a desperate mother is in hiding with her little girl. The last thing she needs is her nosy Texas Ranger neighbor getting friendly....*

Alex raised her gaze, starting to say something, but then she froze like a possum in oncoming headlights.

"Mrs. Hunt? Everything okay?"

She eyed the encircled silver star pinned to his denim button-down shirt. He'd been working this morning and hadn't bothered to remove the badge. "Interesting symbol," she said slowly.

"Represents the Texas Rangers."

"L-like the baseball team?"

"No, ma'am. Like the law enforcement agency." Maybe that would make her feel safer about her temporary new surroundings. He jerked his thumb toward his house. "You have a bona fide lawman living right next door."

Beneath the freckles, her face went whiter than his hat. "Really? That's…" She gave herself a quick shake. "Come on, Belle. Inside now. Before, um, before that mud stains."

"Okay." Belle hung her head but rallied long enough to add, "Bye-bye, Mister Zane. I hope I get to pet Dolly again soon."

From Alex's behavior, Zane had a suspicion they wouldn't be getting together for neighborly potluck dinners anytime in the near future. Instead of commenting on the kid's likelihood of seeing Dolly again, he waved. "Bye, Belle. Stay fabulous."

She beamed. "I will!"

Then mother and daughter disappeared into the house, the front door banging shut behind them.

"Is there something about me," he asked Dolly, "that makes females want to slam doors?"

The only response he got from the dog was an impatient tug on her leash. "Right. I promised you a walk." They started again down the sidewalk, but he found himself periodically glancing over his shoulder and pondering his new neighbors. Cute kid, but she seemed like a handful. And Alex Hunt, once she'd calmed from her mama-bear fury, was perhaps the most skittish woman he'd ever met. If she were a horse, she'd have to wear blinders to keep from jumping at her own shadow. Zane wondered if there was a Mr. Hunt in the picture.

Be sure to look for RESCUED BY A RANGER
by Tanya Michaels in September 2012 from
Harlequin® American Romance®!